Blinded by Love

By Reana Malori

Reana Malori

CONTENTS

Prologue
Chapter 1
Chapter 2
Chapter 3
Chapter 4
Chapter 5
Chapter 6
Chapter 7
Chapter 8
Chapter 9
Chapter 10
Chapter 11
Chapter 12
Chapter 13
Chapter 14
Chapter 15
Chapter 16
Chapter 17
Chapter 18
Chapter 19
Chapter 20
Chapter 21
Chapter 22
Epilogue

More Love Vixen Books
Thank You!
Ruthless Bachelor – Excerpt
About the Author
Also by Reana Malori

Blinded by Love

Summary

Dear Love Vixen,

I don't know what to do and I need your help! My best friend died one year ago. Since then, I've been helping her husband with their five-year-old daughter. I didn't mean for it to happen but… I've fallen in love with my best friend's husband.

I'm so torn. Do women have a 'Sister Code' that says we can't date an ex? Because if there is, I think I'm about to break that rule in a huge way. I'd love nothing more than to climb him like a spider-monkey, but I'm worried that I'm betraying my friend's memory.

Please help me, Love Vixen. My feelings for him seem so wrong, but I can't just turn them off. Do I keep my feelings to myself and just deal with my own heartbreak? Should I let him know how I feel? Should I just suck it up and find someone else?

Sincerely,
Confused in Virginia

*****

Dear Virginia,

Oh sweetie, you are in a pickle.

Grief has no timeline and he's still mourning. You need to take a step back and focus on his child while he heals. You are a remarkable woman to rearrange your life in order to be there for the little girl. With patience and caring he may one day realize what has been right in front of him.

You asked me what you should do? There isn't an easy answer. Is life ever easy? Listen to your heart. It seems like you already know what to do.

Good luck, hon!
The ♥ Vixen

Prologue

Norah

It wasn't supposed to end this way. The life and memories we'd built together were supposed to last until we were old and gray. Rebecca had been my best friend for most of my life. Since the first day she walked into our 2nd grade classroom. Her blonde ponytail hung low as her face revealed the biggest smile. My hand shot in the air when the teacher asked the class if someone wanted to be Rebecca's buddy. She was going to be my new best friend. After all, we were wearing the same color that day, so our friendship was destined.

And that friendship, that sisterhood, lasted more than twenty-four years. In all my dreams, we would still be laughing together, causing trouble, and being a family until we were old women with no teeth.

The woman lying in bed with IV lines and tubes sticking out of her body was not the woman I'm used to seeing. Her frail body looked so small in that hospital bed. My nostrils picked up that distinctive odor of antiseptic, bleach, and sickness. My body was primed and ready to run away from it all. Maybe this was all one long-ass nightmare. Wetness trailed down my face as I prayed with every ounce of my soul that my best friend would survive. It didn't matter what the doctors said. What the hell did they know anyway?

"Stop standing over there sulking," Rebecca called out to me. "I hear you thinking all the way over here, and I need you to stop."

Pulling away from the entrance to her bedroom, I shuffled over to the bed. "I don't sulk."

Rebecca grinned as she tried to sit up. Jumping in to help, I fluffed the pillow behind her back. "What are you doing? You should be resting."

"Stop fussing over me, Norah," she said in a raspy voice. "You are such a worrywart."

I sighed before sitting down in the chair next to her bed. "I'm not. I just..." I stopped speaking, the tears clogging up my throat. "Rebecca, I can't lose you," I whispered.

Leaning her head back, Rebecca closed her eyes and took a deep breath before turning her head to look at me. "I'm not going anywhere. You've been my best friend since I was knee-high to a grasshopper. Do you think I'm ever going to leave you?"

Both of us laughed at her grasshopper comment. Although she had moved to Virginia when Rebecca was young, some of the favorite phrases from her southern belle mother still escaped. Of course, that was one of her favorite sayings, along with telling everyone how me and Rebecca were two peas in a pod. She swore God must have sent us down to earth at the same time so we could find each other in this life.

Looking at the pale, almost translucent skin of my best friend, I wondered how the hell I'd ever live without her again. What was I supposed to do now?

"Where's Lilly? Cade?"

Glancing over my shoulder, I motioned with my thumb. "He took her out for a walk. I swear, he practically ran out of here as soon as I showed up. No words, just a grunt as he passed me by."

She laughed before her breath left, and her body was wracked with deep coughs. "Don't make me laugh. It hurts."

Lifting a glass of water, I placed it against Rebecca's lips. "I'm sorry."

"Don't be." She leaned back and took a few deep breaths. "Listen. Don't worry about Cade. He just..." she paused, "he's been worried about me. He's been using all his time and every resource at his disposal. I tried to tell him to stop focusing on what he can't control and to just make sure Lilly knows how much I love her. I wish I didn't have to leave him alone."

I couldn't help the tears that flowed down my face. The love Rebecca felt for her family could not be denied. Ever since their wedding, more than seven years ago, all I could do was watch Rebecca build a life with the man who'd stolen my friend's heart.

"I'm not worried about Cade. I'm worried about Lilly. She's my goddaughter."

Rebecca nodded before taking a deep breath. "Then you need to be around her more."

My heart seized at her words. She was asking too much of me. "I can't, Rebecca."

"Why? Tell me one good reason why you can't be around more. In the last few years, I've seen you maybe four to six times a year."

Watching my best friend pause as she gathered her breath and her thoughts, I couldn't help but think I should be the one lying in that bed. No husband. No children. My life is my job. Yes, I'm close to my family, but it's not the same.

"Norah? Tell me what's going on with you."

There was no way in hell I was going to tell her a damn thing, especially with her fighting for her life. "Nothing's going on with me. You know how work is for me. I'm always busy."

Rebecca shook her head. "Nope. You work from home. You're a consultant and make your own hours. Try again."

"Why are you pushing so hard on this? You know I see you and Lilly when I can. And no matter how much we see each other, or not, you're still my best friend and my sister. Nothing will change that." I needed her to know that I would always love her. Other than my parents, she was the only person who meant a damn to me. Well, her and Lilly. That mini-me version of my best friend held a piece of my heart.

"Norah," she said in a low voice. "You know why I'm pushing." She sighed deeply while grabbing my hand in hers. "He's going to need you."

There was no reason to ask who she was talking about. We both knew. "I don't think he'll agree with you on that. That man can't even be in the same room as me for more than three minutes."

A smile lit up Rebecca's face. "Stop it. You know I'm right. He's going to need you, and Lilly will need her aunt Norah more than ever. So, I need you to promise me you'll take care of them. Yes, that includes Cade."

I could do nothing but shake my head as the tears flowed. "I can't. Don't ask me to do that. You're gonna fight this. All you need is a bit more time," I said, squeezing her hand tighter than I probably should. "You sound like you're giving up, which I know you're not going to do. You have to stay with me. You can't leave us."

Eyes closing, Rebecca's words were slower as she began to fall asleep. "The fight isn't over yet, but I'm tired, Norah. No matter what happens, you're my sister. I trust you more than anything. I know you'll take care of them."

***

Fuck cancer.

Fuck cancer in its rotten, life-taking ass.

Those were the only words I could think of as we stood in the rain while Rebecca's coffin was lowered into the ground. There were so many people here—her work colleagues, family, friends, and neighbors. Everyone loved Rebecca, but no one loved her like I did. We'd experienced our entire life together. Puberty. Acne. Our first bra. First boyfriends. First heartbreaks. College.

Everything. Good, bad, and in between. Every pivotal moment of their lives was spent with each other. When Rebecca married Cade, there was no reason to think things would be different. But if I were honest with myself, I knew from the start how this would play out. The moment Cade and Rebecca became a serious couple, things would change. There would be no other choice.

Cade and Lilly were sitting next to me. The little girl sat between us as she cried into her father's chest. My instinct was to reach over and pull the small child into my arms, but I resisted. Cade's grip on Lilly was tight, as if he'd never let her go. I couldn't blame him. He'd just lost his wife and the mother of his child. Glancing up at him, the expression on his face stopped me cold. He looked straight ahead, but I could see the tears welling in his eyes.

When Rebecca had been diagnosed with Stage 4 pancreatic cancer, it had thrown everyone for a loop. Most of all, her husband. From the date of diagnosis until the day she passed away in his arms, it had been just over one year. She'd gotten a late-stage diagnosis, and by then, none of the treatments worked. Chemotherapy. Alternative medicine. Everything. Nothing. After all they'd tried, it was all for nothing. Rebecca was still gone. Cade was without a wife. Lilly no longer had a mother.

I was without my best friend. My sister. The only person who understood me.

What was I supposed to do now?

It was time for me to go home. I'd been coming back and forth to Falls Church to visit Rebecca for the past year. Shortly after Rebecca's wedding, I'd moved to Baltimore. It was the best decision for everyone. Especially me.

My heart squeezed with pain and guilt at what I'd done.

I hadn't been there for my best friend because of something I could never admit to her, no matter how much it pained me to stay away. There was no other choice. The alternative was not an option.

"Let's go," Cade said.

I jerked at his words, my mind coming back to the present situation. Unfortunately, I'd been so lost in my thoughts, I'd failed to realize that Rebecca's casket was in the ground, and the crowd had begun to disperse.

"I'm sorry," I said, looking into his green eyes. "What was that?"

"Food's back at the house. People will expect us there." As I continued to stare at him, he shook his head and picked up his daughter in his arms. "Are you coming or what?"

His words were a harsh reminder that he could barely stand being around me. Good. That was for the best. Maybe I could go home now and not be around Cade anymore. My heart was already broken, and my friend was no longer here. I could plan to see Lilly on the weekends, kind of like joint custody.

With one last lingering look at the gravesite, I made my way over to the car waiting for me on the street.

"I'm sorry, Rebecca. I'll miss you so much, but I can't stay here. Not with him. I'll take care of Lilly as best I can, but...." I paused to take a deep breath, "I need to stay away from your husband. If I don't, I'm going to do something foolish, and I could never betray you like that."

With one last lingering look, I made my way over to Cade and Lilly. Once there, I reached for Lilly. Cade handed her over, and we climbed into the black limousine. Cradling Lilly's head on my shoulder, I sat in the far corner of the vehicle waiting for Cade to slide his tall form into the car. As we rode in silence, I couldn't help looking over at the man sitting next to me.

Cade wasn't a pretty man, but his looks could captivate a room. Short, dark hair covered his head, and his thick dark beard was neat and trimmed. The dark suit fit his form like a second skin. Everything about Cade screamed power. From the first moment I laid eyes on him more than eight years ago, I had been drawn to him.

That hadn't changed over the years, which made me the worst kind of person.

No matter how much I tried to fight it, I was in love with the man sitting next to me. How could I do this to Rebecca?

With that thought, I knew it was time for me to leave. I needed to get away from this city and far away from Cade.

Chapter 1

Norah

One Year Later

"Norah, you need to come back."

As I listened to Cade's voicemail, I could feel my body tensing. I'd just made it home from spending the weekend with him and Lilly. My body was tired. My heart was hurting. Being around them for more than two or three days brought me close to my breaking point. When I was with them, all I could think about was Rebecca. She should be the one there with them. Not me.

Yet, I also couldn't help feeling as if I were right where I belonged.

Then he had to go and send me this damn voicemail. Collapsing on my living room couch, I looked around my empty apartment and sighed. My house reflected how I felt inside. Bare. No personality. Minimalist. I had survived this way for so long. It felt like this was all I knew. This was my real life. Not the one I pretended to have when I was with Cade and Lilly.

Hitting the replay button on my phone, I listened to his entire message again.

"Norah, you need to come back. Lilly won't stop crying. It's becoming too difficult for her when you leave. You're her godmother. I don't know why Rebecca chose you for the job when clearly you have no desire to step up," he paused. Then I heard him take a few deep breaths. "You need to be here with Lilly. I expect a return call."

Asshole!

What did my best friend see in him anyway? All he did was bark orders, especially at me. With Lilly, he was different. Then again, maybe that was it all along. I was simply his late wife's best friend. To him, I was nothing, which is how he treated me; like the hired help.

Of course, I wanted to be there with Lilly. Hearing her cry for her mom at night broke my heart. All I could do was hold her in my arms and tell her that I loved her, and make sure she knew that I was there for her. Her beautiful blue eyes, so reminiscent of her mother's, would gaze up at me with tears and doubt. For a small child, the experience of losing her mother must have felt like the end of the world. Then here I come, showing up on the weekends with smiles, doing all the things a mother would do, then I would dash away, leaving her alone for the entire week.

Glancing around my house again, I could feel the tears welling in my eyes. It wasn't because I didn't want to be around her. No, that wasn't it at all. I was a damn coward.

There, I said it. All things considered, I knew I was doing the right thing. Right?

Cade was probably waiting for me to call, but he'd have to wait a bit longer. Earlier, when his call came through, I was still on the road from Falls Church to Baltimore. Yes, it was petty, and I chose not to pick up. He'd called three times. The voicemail was left after his final attempt to reach me.

Standing, I walked into the kitchen and grabbed a bottle of water. Just thinking about the look on his face when I climbed in my car had me shivering all over. Why did I have to be this drawn to him? Not once during their marriage had I even considered overstepping. Then again, that's also one of the reasons I stopped visiting so much. When I wanted to see Rebecca, we arranged to meet at a neutral place, or she came to me. It was always easier to make the excuse that we needed a girl's weekend. No boys allowed.

Unpacking my weekend suitcase, I threw the clothes in the wash. Then I made something to eat since I hadn't stopped on the road. Glancing over at the clock, I'd been home thirty minutes and still hadn't returned Cade's call. Okay, fine. I didn't want to talk to him. Remember what I said earlier? Yeah, I feel like a complete coward.

"Ugh. Fine!" I yelled out into the empty room. I picked up my phone and clicked on his name to push through a call. I'd now switched to a glass of wine because a girl needed some extra liquid courage. After two rings, he picked up.

"Are you on the way back?"

He could be such an asshole. "Wow! Well, hello to you, too. Yes, I made it home safely. Thanks so much for asking."

His deep sigh came through the other side of the line. "Clearly, you're safe because you called me. Why do you act like this? Never mind. So, when are you coming back?"

How do I handle this? On the one hand, I needed space. He had no idea how I felt about him, and that was for the best. He'd be appalled and disgusted. Hell, I was halfway disgusted myself.

"Cade, I'll be back next Friday night. That was the arrangement. We agreed to that. Why are you changing the rules?"

"Hold on," he grumbled into the phone.

I heard sounds on the other side of the line, as if he were shifting around. "Were you asleep?" I looked over at the clock, and it was only a little past nine. Wasn't that a bit early?

"Not asleep. Just lying down and reading some reports. I finally got Lilly down to sleep after she spent two hours crying for her auntie Norah to return. Do you know how it feels to hear her crying for you? Don't you think she's been through enough? She can't take much more of you leaving her right when she needs you the most. My daughter doesn't deserve this."

My first reaction was anger that he was blaming me. My second reaction was hurt. It was never my intention to make things worse for Lilly. I thought the weekends with me would be enough. That having me around, even for that little time, would help her get through. Maybe I was wrong.

"I'm not sure what you're trying to say—" Cade interrupts me before I can continue.

"You need to shit or get off the pot. You're her godmother. Rebecca wanted you to be there for Lilly if something ever happened to her. Well, it has. My wife is gone. Your best friend," he spat out, "is gone. Her daughter needs you. So, what are you going to do? Keep running? Hide away from everyone who needs you? That's what you do best, right? Run? Well,

I won't let you. Next time you come back to house, then you're here to stay."

"Man, you have lost your damn mind." Now, I'm seething. If I was a dragon, you'd see fire coming from my mouth right now. He was so arrogant and controlling. How did Rebecca deal with his insufferable ass? "You don't get to tell me what to do. I'm not your wife."

"Yeah, I know. You're nothing like Rebecca. She was light and sweet and everything that was right in this world. You are most definitely NOT my wife."

My response to his words caught in my throat. What was I supposed to say to that? No, I wasn't his wife. Rebecca brought out the best in everyone she was around. Whenever I was sad, she could bring a smile to my face with just a few words. I was still in a state of shock when he continued speaking.

"Listen, Norah. I'm—I'm—"

In all the time I'd known him, he'd never apologized to me for anything. This was a momentous day.

"If you're unwilling to help me full-time with Lilly, then maybe it's best if you don't come around at all."

Skkrrrrtt!! Wait. What did he just say? Did I hear him wrong? "Excuse me?"

"You heard me. I can't have Lilly crying herself to sleep every night when you're not here. My daughter is everything to me. She's all I have left of Rebecca. If you can't be here for her the way she needs, then maybe it's better if you don't visit for a while. I need her to have stability. She needs people who will choose to be around. Losing her mother was out of her control, and she doesn't understand it."

"I know that!" I couldn't help but yell through the phone. "Do you think I wanted to watch my friend die? Rebecca should be here with us. I wasn't expecting this. My life is here in Baltimore." I had to repeat the words because they had to be true. My life wasn't with them. It couldn't be. There was no way in hell I could step in and be a full-time surrogate mom. That's not how I was built.

"Then I guess I have my answer."

This dude was like a dog with a bone. "No, I haven't given you an answer yet. Cade, what am I supposed to do about my life here?"

"If I recall, you're a consultant. You can work from anywhere. This house is large enough for you to have your own office for work. Norah, I'm not going to beg you to come back here to help Lilly. I'm simply telling you what she needs. If you can't be there for us... for her, then don't come back. If you show up at my doorstep, then I'll take that as a sign that you're here for good."

He honestly had no idea what he was asking me to do.

"Cade..."

"If you need to think about it that much, then it seems you've made your decision. Goodbye, Norah." He hung up the phone, and I sat there in silence as I thought over his request... no, his demand.

That man acted as if I owed him something. I didn't.

No, but I did owe something to Rebecca. She'd trusted me to be there for her daughter. So how could I not do what Cade asked? I'd already noticed that every time I left, Lilly became a little more inconsolable. Her tears would fall faster and harder as she watched me climb into my car for the long drive home every week.

I wanted to be there for Lilly. I needed to be there for her, but what would it do to me, my own peace of mind, if I stayed in the house with them every day?

You know what? Maybe I needed to stop being so damn selfish. This was not about me. This was not about my own skewed feelings for a man that I could never have. Maybe the best thing I could do was just focus on myself and Lilly. Living with them would be no big deal, right?

My work could be done from anywhere. My apartment lease would continue until I returned, maybe. He didn't say how long he wanted me to stay with them, but I'm positive it would only be a couple of months. At least until Lilly was able to sleep at night. I could totally do this.

Although I was going to take him up on his proposal, I wanted to make his ass sweat a little longer. The man was just plain rude. Ever since I'd known him, he always seemed to get what he wanted. Sure, I'd do this for him, but it would be on my terms. If he stayed out of my way, I'd be fine. Right?

I could feel my eyes drooping as a wave of exhaustion came over me. Time to go to bed. I'd worry about Cade and his demands tomorrow. Right now, I needed sleep.

Chapter 2

Cade

"I don't want to go to school, Daddy."

My precious angel's voice was so loud I heard it over the buzz of my electric razor. Not this again. I flipped off the switch, and the room was briefly plunged into silence. Turning to look at the little girl standing at my bathroom door, I wanted to smile, but that would send a message that her behavior was okay. It wasn't.

"Sweetheart, you have to go to school. That's what little kids do. They go to school and learn."

"No. I want auntie Norah."

This time she stomped her foot, which was something her mother had done on more than one occasion when she was angry. Every day, she reminded me more and more of my sweet Rebecca. Without warning, I felt my heart clench as I thought of her no longer being here with us. How was I supposed to do this without her?

Squatting down so that I was face-to-face with my little girl, I grabbed her hand. "She had to go home, sweetheart. Remember how we explained that auntie Norah lives in Baltimore, which is very far away. She'll be here every single weekend to make sure you get special time with her. But one thing I do know is that she would want you to go to school."

When her bottom lip started to tremble, I knew I was lost. My brain told me I shouldn't give in to her, but my heart couldn't help but feel for my little girl. Her entire world had been turned upside down. My mother had stayed for a while, but she was too old to run after a five-year-old little girl. She came over as much as she could, but I couldn't ask her to keep on doing that.

Then what makes you think you can tell Norah to give up her life?

Yeah, I was wrong for that, but it wouldn't change my mind. Norah was Lilly's godmother, which meant she was the person Rebecca had intended to be there for her daughter if something happened. Well, it did happen, and Norah needed to show up. No more half-assing things. If she couldn't be here with Lilly to help her get through this, then she needed to stay the hell away from his daughter.

"Daddy, why are you looking like that?"

Lilly's voice broke into my thoughts. "What do you mean?" I stood back up and walked out of the bathroom. Another day working from home. It was fine. I was the boss. I could work from home every single day if I wanted to. For me, it was the principle. Being in the office showed my employees that I was right there with them, holding things down, attending meetings, making the calls that needed to be made.

But this situation was different. I knew everyone understood what was happening, but I also didn't want anyone's pity.

"Waffles?" I asked Lilly.

"Pancakes!"

"You got it. Go ahead and sit at the table while I cook your breakfast." I also needed to make a call to the office. Picking up my phone, I dialed the number for Mildred. The woman was almost old enough to be my mother, but she ran the office with an iron fist. Nothing got past her. Hell, half the people in the office were afraid to cross her. The other half knew she was really the one keeping the trains running and just got on board. That was a good thing. She was the last line of defense before people were able to get to me. I was glad she took her job seriously, and as a result, I paid her handsomely.

"Morning, Mr. Donovan," she answered the phone.

"How'd you know it was me?"

"You're the only one who calls my private line this early in the morning. Everything okay with Ms. Lilly?"

Yup, this woman knew everything. "No. Today's not a good day. I'll be working from home. Anything on my calendar that I can't miss?"

"You have a meeting with that security company, Overwatch. They want to partner with you about doing some executive assessments on potential clients. Other than that, everything can be handled by other people."

That meeting with Overwatch was important. It could get me into a market that I'd been trying to break into for a while. Those guys were hired by some of the most prominent figures in the world. It would launch my business to the next level. I couldn't miss this meeting.

"Is the meeting in-person or virtual?" There had to be a way I could do this.

"Looks like a virtual meeting. Want me to cancel, or can you make it?"

Hell yeah, I could make it. "I'll be there. Did you email me the bios of the owners?"

"Yes, the document with the information is waiting for you in your email. Anything else?"

I almost laughed at how she was rushing me off the phone. You'd think she was the one running the company and not me. Okay, maybe she was. "Nothing else. Thanks, Mildred. Oh, wait, one more thing. Can you get me the name and number for a highly reputable nanny service?"

Her laughter came through the phone. "What happened to the other young lady you had watching Lilly? I think her name was Catie, right?"

I scratched my head. I didn't want to think about how that had ended last week. "Yeah, she's no longer a viable option. I need someone who cares about their job rather than getting to me."

I hated to admit that when Catie first started watching Lilly, I'd breathed a sigh of relief. She seemed perfect, even if a little in awe of the house. So, it was no big deal that she spent more time talking to me in the mornings and at night when I came home rather than focusing on Lilly. I had no idea that Lilly meant it when she said she didn't like Catie. I mean, she *really* meant it.

Then last Friday, when I'd come home early, she was lying in my bed naked while my daughter was by herself in the playroom. I got her out of my house as fast as I could and called the agency to let them know she should never come back to my home. Less than ten minutes after Catie ran out of the house crying, embarrassed, and apologizing, Norah had shown up.

I would hate for Norah to show up and find some young twenty-something half-naked in my house. One reason is, I'm not over my wife and I sure as hell wasn't looking to replace her with a girl barely out of college. The second reason was harder to admit, but I didn't want Norah to think poorly of me.

She already thought I was too rough around the edges and no good for her friend Rebecca. Not that she'd ever said that to my face, but I'd heard them talking after a few months of Rebecca and I dating. I'll never forget those words.

"Rebecca, don't you think he's a little too much for you? I mean, this guy has tattoos all over his body. He looks more like a biker than a CEO. Just… be careful, okay?"

"Don't worry, Norah. He's good for me. He's a good man. Don't let his looks fool you. Plus, he's usually the kind of guy you would go for. You like them rough and tough and bad."

"Is he bad, Rebecca? Actually, don't answer that. Listen, I want you to be happy. If he makes you smile every day, then I'm all for it. He's lucky to have you."

"Your Prince Charming is right around the corner. Maybe you should stop working so dang hard and focus on having some fun. You can't find your Mr. Right if you're not looking."

There was a pause before Norah spoke again. "Even when I find him, he's not interested. I'm okay, girl. Now, let's get back to the party before your man comes looking for you."

I'd been able to back away before they'd seen me standing there snooping around. Up until that time, I thought Norah was supportive of our relationship. Not that she'd ever been outright rude or dismissive, but she'd always looked so happy when we were all together.

I could admit that when I'd seen the two of them at the top of the W Hotel in DC, I was intrigued by Norah first. She'd been wearing a shimmery silver dress that hugged her curves. The back of her dress dipped low, and I saw that she wasn't wearing a bra. As I looked her up and down, her toned, brown legs made me look twice. When she turned to the side, I caught a glimpse of her face. After that, nothing could have stopped me from taking a step forward. I was intent on speaking with her and seeing where things could go.

However, just as I moved closer, Rebecca stepped in front of me. Her blonde hair, blue eyes, and sweet voice pulled at another part of me. She was the one who spoke first. Distracted for a moment, I lost sight of Norah until she approached Rebecca and me a few minutes later. That's when I found out they were friends. After a quick glance at her friend's hand on my chest, Norah smiled. A man had come up to her, pulling her attention away… and that was that.

If, but for an extra second, Norah would have been the one I spent the entire night talking to, falling in love with, and marrying.

But it hadn't been her, and I could honestly admit that I loved Rebecca more than I ever thought I could. She saw all the good in me even when I couldn't see it in myself. Being with her made me a better man. She'd been the perfect wife, mother, and lover for the entirety of our relationship.

Who cares if she never argued with me? Whenever I raised my voice, it felt like I'd just kicked a puppy.

It didn't matter that our love life, while damn good, still felt lacking in some ways. See, all those years ago, when Norah had tried to warn Rebecca that I was too much for her, she was right.

Nice and gentle wasn't in my vocabulary before Rebecca. My nature was to be rough and hard. The first time I'd tried to unleash the full extent of my desires in the bedroom, I could feel the uncertainty coming from Rebecca. So, I'd stopped, and I never tried to do it again.

Our lovemaking was always gentle and soft, with words of passion and love falling from our lips. I loved my wife because she loved me so deeply in return. There was nothing I wouldn't do for her, even if it meant pushing down my need for something more. What we had together was good. Hell, it was great. If she'd lived for another fifty years, there was no doubt I would have continued loving her and being the man she needed me to be.

That didn't mean I didn't wonder about an alternate future.

Which only made me hate myself even more. My wife deserved the best of me. She deserved a man who would honor her memory without questioning why she'd been the one he married. A feeling of betrayal filled my stomach, and I didn't like that shit at all. I'd been a faithful husband to Rebecca. Not once had I ever considered stepping out on her. She was perfect. I was the one who wasn't good enough for her.

"Daddy! Daddy! Are the pancakes done yet?"

Broken from my traitorous thoughts, I glanced over at my daughter. Rebecca may be gone, but I still had one of the best parts of her sitting at the table, staring up at me with eyes so much like hers, it caused my heart to stutter.

"Almost. While we wait, why don't you run through the alphabet for me."

"Okay. A… B… C…"

The only person I had to focus on was the little girl sitting at the kitchen table waiting for breakfast. Young twenty-somethings couldn't do a damn thing for me. If the time came and I needed an itch scratched, I'd take care of it. But right now, all I needed was to get through today, then I'd worry about tomorrow.

Chapter 3

Norah

It wasn't Friday, but I figured why wait? After Cade's call on Sunday, I spent the next few days getting things in order, which wasn't much. I had no office I needed to shut down or employees I needed to answer to. There was only me myself and I. It was a sad existence, but it was still mine.

With too much time on my hands, I started listening to some of the podcasts I'd bookmarked. The Love Vixen had a blog also, but everyone was raving about her podcast. The thing was, she was a relationship guru of some type. Women, and some men, reached out to her from all over the world. Every one of them wanted her guidance on a relationship dilemma. I mean, some of the letters she received were so crazy. What type of woman sent in a letter to a strange woman, if she was one, spilling their guts about their love life?

I did.

I was that type of woman.

Two days after my disastrous call with Cade, I caved.

Dear Love Vixen,

I don't know what to do and I need your help! My best friend died one year ago. Since then, I've been helping her husband with their five-year-old daughter. I didn't mean for it to happen, but... I've fallen in love with my best friend's husband.

I'm so torn. Do women have a 'Sister Code' that says we can't date an ex? Because if there is, I think I'm about to break that rule in a huge way. I'd love nothing more than to climb him like a spider monkey, but I'm worried that I'm betraying my friend's memory.

Please help me, Love Vixen. My feelings for him seem so wrong, but I can't just turn them off. Do I keep my feelings to myself and just deal with my own heartbreak? Should I let him know how I feel? Should I just suck it up and find someone else?

Sincerely,

Confused in Virginia

I was confused, alright. And I was a damn fool. Well, it was too late to do anything about it now. She'd either respond or not, but it felt good to get those crazy thoughts out of my head and on paper. So, here I stood on a bright sunny Wednesday morning. I could have used my key to open the door, but I thought that might be a bit presumptuous.

Cade's car was still in the driveway, so I knew he was home. I'd intentionally planned to arrive before he had to leave for the office. I just hoped that nanny Catie wasn't here. Every time I came to the house, she looked at me sideways. As if I were intruding. Little did she know that I had more rights to be in this house than any woman. Ringing the doorbell again, I waited for him to open the door. I turned when I heard the lock disengage.

"What? Shit. Norah? What are you doing here?"

Such a sunny disposition. "Good morning to you too. Are you going to let me in?"

Stepping back, he glared at me as I crossed the threshold. "Why didn't you just use your damn key? You know how crazy things get around here in the morning."

Setting my bag down on the floor, I rotated my neck to work out the kinks. I'd woken up at five o'clock to make it here before eight. "You weren't expecting me. What if you thought I was an intruder or something? Knocking was better."

I saw him glance down at my bag and his gaze captured mine. "So, does this mean what I think it does? You finally here to stay?"

I removed my shoes and placed them along the wall next to his larger ones and Lilly's smaller ones. There were shoes just a little smaller than mine, also next to Cade's. They belonged to Rebecca. Seeing that gave me proof that I was doing the right thing. I needed to be here for Lilly, but Cade was not mine. No matter that I'd sent that stupid submission to The Love Vixen, I had to stay in control.

"That's what it looks like. You gave me an ultimatum. Either I come here to stay full-time, or I give up seeing Lilly. That's not something I'm willing to do."

He stared at me. I glared at him. This time, I wasn't willing to back down. If he had something to say, then he needed to open his mouth and do that.

"Is Lilly still getting dressed?"

"No, I was planning to work from home again today, so she's in her pajamas."

I'd already started to walk into the kitchen when his words stopped me. "What do you mean she's still in her pajamas? Doesn't she have school today?"

He shrugged before finally closing and locking the front door. "She's in kindergarten. What is there to learn? We go over her ABC's here, we study her numbers, and I bought her a ton of workbooks she can use to pass the time."

I shook my head at him. "She needs other kids, Cade. Socialization. Learning how to deal with other people even when life sucks. You can't keep her at home every day, and you need to go into the office."

"She's fine. I'm fine. I've already told Mildred that I'm working from home this week. I wasn't sure if you'd be coming back, so I've been interviewing nannies."

At that, I paused. "What happened to Catie?"

Red began coloring his cheeks. "She was no longer working out."

"Is that all?" I'd seen the way she looked at him.

"Yes," he barked before turning and walking deeper into the house.

That wasn't all there was to that situation, but I'd let it go for now. "Okay, well, we'll still need a dependable nanny. There'll be times when I need to visit clients, and we'll need to make sure someone is here for Lilly." He didn't respond to me, even though I knew he heard every word I said. "I need to see the profiles for any of the women you're considering."

"None of them were good enough. I'm still looking."

I looked at him as he stood there awkwardly, and I couldn't help the smile that came over my face. "All of them seem more interested in the father rather than the daughter?"

He let out an exasperated breath. "I mean, how do other single fathers do it? Some of these women are so blatant, it makes my skin crawl. Mildred said she contacted the absolute best agency in the city, but none of them have felt right. They eyeball me like I'm on the menu. All I want is someone who can take care of my daughter. Why is this so damn hard?"

He stood in front of me, hands on his jean-clad hips and a tight black t-shirt stretched across his chest and arms. His arm tattoos were visible. I could see the top of his chest and neck tats. The man was a walking, talking sex magnet. Until he opened his mouth and something rude fell out. But still…

"Do you really have no clue?"

"What?"

If he didn't know, I sure as hell wasn't going to tell him. "Nope. I'm not doing this with you. Where's my baby?"

Lifting one arm, he motioned for me to walk ahead of him. "She's in the kitchen waiting on me to cook breakfast."

I passed him quickly, walked toward the back of the house where the kitchen was located, and snuck up behind Lilly. She was so concentrated on her workbook, she hadn't picked up on my voice while talking to her father. "Surprise," I yelled out.

She turned around in her seat, her face lighting up with a huge smile. "Auntie Norah! You're here. I knew you were coming back. I told Dad you would be back. I missed you. I don't want to go to school. Can we have pancakes every morning? Are you going to read me a bedtime story every night?"

Gathering up the little girl in my arms, I lifted her so I could walk further into the room full of natural light. There was a cushioned bench situated against one wall. Rebecca and I would sit there when she was ill, and I was here visiting the house. It was our special spot to talk about our life adventures, regrets, and the memories that would never leave us. I sat down on the bench, with Lilly resting on my lap, and enjoyed the moment. I saw Cade walk into the kitchen and step up to the stove from the corner of my eye.

That's the one thing that surprised me about him. When Rebecca told me he cooked most of their meals, I didn't believe her. Here was a man with a whole lot of money, with everything he wanted at his disposal. He'd bought a mini-mansion with five bedrooms, two living rooms, a pool, a large backyard, and every amenity money can buy. Yet, he cooked full-ass meals for breakfast and dinner daily. It didn't fit the image of him that I had in my head.

When I spent my first weekend here with them about a year after they married, there he was, making breakfast fit for a King or Queen in the kitchen since he rarely ate what he cooked. Usually, he was always off to a meeting of some sort. That day, when he was finished cooking, he'd kissed Rebecca before leaving to meet up with some buddies.

Thinking back, it had been the damndest thing, but it turns out, the man just loved cooking. He loved cooking for his wife and then his daughter once she was born. It went against everything I thought about him. Wasn't he supposed to be an overly macho man who wouldn't dare step foot in the kitchen or touch a dish? Well, he definitely didn't clean, because they had someone come in twice a week to handle the household chores. With Rebecca working full-time as a marketing manager, that was a blessing. Then after Lilly was born, she began working from home full-time so she could be there with their little one. It had been the type of life my friend had always wanted. I couldn't be happier that she was able to live the life of her dreams with a man she loved.

Then cancer came in and wiped it all away.

"Auntie Norah. Are you gonna leave again?" Lilly asked, breaking me away from my memories. Her small hands cradled my face as she looked at me with such innocence and trust.

I shook my head. "No, Lilly Ladybug. I'm not leaving again. I'm here to stay. Know why?"

Lilly shook her head. "No. Why?"

Glancing over at Cade, I could see him listening intently to our conversation. Maybe he also needed to be reassured because I know this situation wasn't easy for him either.

Turning to Lilly, I smiled. "Because I miss you too much when I'm gone. I don't ever want to be away from you again. So, I'm here with you to make sure you get your baths at night and to read you a story and to talk about whatever you want." As I said that last little bit, my lip trembled. I knew the subject of her mother would come up because it always did. Lilly wanted to know all about her mother. She seemed hungry to hear everything she could, especially now that Rebecca was no longer here.

"You promise? You won't leave me?" she asked, those blue eyes staring at me with hope and a little bit of fear.

I nodded, trying to manage a smile. "Nope. Never again. I'm here to stay. You're my ladybug, and I need to be here with you. No matter what." I looked over at Cade to find him staring at Lilly and me with an indecipherable look on his face.

"Are you hungry, Norah?" he asked.

I nodded at him. "Yeah, I could eat." I turned to smile at Lilly again, and I crossed my eyes and puffed out my cheeks, making her smile.

"Breakfast will be done in fifteen minutes," Cade called out. After a pause, I heard him speak again in a lower tone. "I'm glad you came back."

All I could do was nod in response. If I opened my mouth to speak, I had no idea what type of confessions and secrets would come spilling out. I wanted to say was that I was happy I was back also. That I was glad to be here with the two of them, that they were my family now because Rebecca was my family. I would take care of them as best I could. I knew I couldn't say any of that because if I did, I was positive he'd hear the longing in my voice—the need in my words. So, I stayed silent. It was best. He wasn't mine. He would never be mine.

So, my wishful thinking needed to be buried deep, locked away, and the key thrown into the woods, never to be seen again.

Chapter 4

Cade

Norah shouldn't be here.

Truth was, I didn't want her here.

But even though I felt that way, I also knew that I needed her here.

Watching Norah with Lilly brought a smile to my face. It had been too many days and weeks since I'd seen my little girl so happy. Hell, it had been much longer than that. She'd been so worried about her mother being sick that her beautiful smile had started to fade. That's not something that should happen to a five-year-old little girl. Her smile should be the largest thing about her.

She'd lost that for a moment, but today… it was back.

No, Norah shouldn't be here. My wife should be sitting on the bench with our little girl waiting for me to make them breakfast. Rebecca should be the one making our daughter smile. This wasn't how it should be.

Rebecca was no longer here. She'd been gone for over a year, but I still missed her every single day. Our talks, her laughter, the way she looked at me as if I hung the moon. All gone. Now, I was only left with the memories of our life together, and it wasn't enough.

Reaching into the fridge, I pulled out the ingredients for breakfast. This is what I know how to do. Take care of the people who meant the most to me. Lilly was a part of me, she was the best part of me, and she would always be the most important person to me.

As my gaze shifted to Norah, I couldn't help but shake my head. We'd never been close, but she'd been part of my life for so long. I knew this was where she needed to be, even as

I fought her presence in my life with everything inside me.

Finishing up the meal, I sat the plates on the table before beckoning them over. "Time to eat."

"Aren't you going to eat?" Norah asked.

I shook my head. "No. I'm good. I had coffee."

"You can't live on coffee every morning. You need to be healthy for Lilly."

For some reason, that got my ire up. "You don't need to tell me what I need to do for my daughter. I'm fine," my voice snapped. Her eyes got wide, as did Lilly's, and I knew it was time for me to step away. Lately, I'd get so caught up with my anger at the situation that I lost focus.

"Don't yell at me, Cade. I'm here because Lilly needs me, but you'd better watch your tone."

Her eyes shot fire at me. For whatever reason, we'd always given each other shit, but I wasn't in the mood this morning. I didn't care that she'd given up her life to come here and help us.

I huffed as I tried to rein in my temper. Lilly was looking at me with shock on her face. In her short life, I can count on one hand the number of times I'd lost my temper in front of her. Especially during the time when Rebecca was sick.

Ignoring the challenge in Norah's eyes, I finished cleaning up the mess in the kitchen. Walking over to the table, I kissed Lilly on the head. "Love you, sweetheart. Daddy will be in the office if you need me. So," I eyed her, "are we going to school today?"

She shook her head at me. "Dad, auntie Norah just got here. I can't go to school today."

I should put my foot down and force her to go, but I just couldn't. She hadn't truly been happy for a long time. Now that Norah was here full-time, I had a feeling her mood would improve. Maybe it was time for me to stop trying to control every situation. Glancing over at Norah, I noticed she was still looking at me with that fierce gaze. "What do you think?"

It took her a few moments to respond. She stopped glaring at me and turned to Lilly. "Sweetheart, you can stay home today, but after that, we need to get you back to school. Deal?"

I watched my daughter nod her head with glee. She hadn't agreed that easily to anything I'd said over the past year. Maybe I should feel jealous, but I wasn't. I'd take the gift she was giving me. Maybe with Lilly back in school regularly, I could get back to the office.

The woman had only been here for an hour, and things were already changing. I wasn't sure if I liked how fast things were moving, but this is what I wanted. Isn't this why I told Norah she needed to return to live with us? Stepping back, I refilled my coffee mug and made to leave the kitchen.

"I'll be in the office if you need me," I mumbled, leaving them to their breakfast.

A chair scraped against the floor, and a second later, I heard Norah calling after me. "Cade? Cade, please stop."

I didn't want to. My body was primed to walk away and get away from her. Maybe it had been the wrong decision asking her to return. Just by being here, she made me remember things I wanted to forget.

"I can't believe you're acting like such an asshole. I just got here. You asked me to come back, Cade. Do you want me to leave?"

That stopped me. Her question pierced me, and my body froze. Her leaving was the one thing I knew I didn't want. Heaving a sigh,

I refused to turn around. “No, I’m not asking you to leave. Lilly needs you here.”

Without looking at her, I could feel her body shifting. She was silent for a few seconds before speaking. “I miss her, too. I miss the sound of her voice when we talk over the phone. Her laugh was so weird, but every time I heard it, I smiled. Just being around her made me feel lighter than I ever thought. She was my best friend, my sister. Every story about every significant moment in my life begins with the words, me and Rebecca. There’s nothing more I want in this world than for her to be here. With Lilly. With you.”

She paused and took a deep breath. I couldn’t turn around, because if I did, she’d see the utter devastation on my face. So, I remained with my back to her.

“I’m sorry that you have me as a sorry substitute for your wife.”

"You're not a substitute for Rebecca. She was my wife. You can't replace her." Even as I heard the words come out of my mouth, I knew they sounded off. No, she wasn't Rebecca. They were very different people. Norah wasn't my wife or Lilly's mother. She couldn't replace Rebecca because that would never be possible, but Norah had her own place in this house, and I knew her love for Lilly was real.

Norah gasped, and I couldn't help but turn to look at her. Eyes shiny with tears, she stared at me with a look of horror on her face. I wanted to reach out to her, to let her know that I wasn't trying to be cruel—that I was just stating a fact. She wasn't here to replace Rebecca, and I didn't want her to feel as if she needed to.

The woman had literally picked up her life and relocated to my home simply because I'd demanded it. She loved my little girl that much and was honoring the memory of her friend. I would always appreciate what she was doing for us, but the hurt and grief were too raw right now. Maybe I hadn't entirely dealt with my wife's passing. Then again, I wasn't ready. I felt as if my heart had been ripped out, leaving a gaping hole where the organ should be.

The only thing keeping me going was my daughter.

I rubbed a hand down my face as I stared at Norah standing in front of me, looking so broken. We'd both gone through hell as we watched Rebecca fade away right in front of our eyes. "Listen, that's not what I meant."

She nodded and interrupted me. "Yes, it is. You meant every word. Just forget about it," she waved a hand at me. "Why don't you keep on going to your office. Lilly is fine with me. I cleared my schedule for the rest of the week, so I could get situated here. And for your information, I would never try to replace Rebecca. You're a sorry motherfucker for saying that to me. How about I stay out of your way, and you stay out of mine? My only purpose is to help that little girl in the other room." She wiped her eyes as she turned away from me and stormed back in the direction of the kitchen.

My feet shifted as if to follow her, but I paused. The last thing I needed was to piss her off more. She wasn't in the mood to hear it, and I honestly didn't know if I had the words in me. Not sure how long I stood there, but when I listened to my daughter's giggle from the other room, something in me relaxed.

Things may not be perfect, but they would be okay. They had to be. There was no other way. Norah being here wasn't ideal, but she was the best option I had for my daughter.

Time to get my head in the game. Work was still waiting for me, so I headed into my home office to focus on that for as long as I could.

Three hours later, I was still sitting in my home office, too distracted to do any real work. Laughter could be heard outside my door. Then again, I hadn't shut it all the way. I wanted to be able to hear Lilly if she needed me. Every so often, I'd hear her childish giggle along with Norah's deeper laugh. They would run through the house, squealing as they played whatever game that had their attention for the moment.

My attention should have been focused on work, but I hadn't gotten much done. If anything, I was less productive today than I'd been before. Neither of them had come in to ask me if I wanted to join them. Not that I would have, but it seemed the courteous thing to do would be to ask. Playing games wasn't my thing, but I enjoyed the occasional moment of hide-and-seek.

Sitting back in my chair, I sighed deeply as I looked over to the chaise lounge that Rebecca had made her own. She'd sit there while I was working, usually reading a book. Because of my job, she didn't need to work, but she was active with Lilly and other social endeavors. I didn't care what she did, as long as she was happy. When she smiled at me, my whole world felt calm. Peaceful.

"I miss you, Rebecca."

It's not that I was expecting her to answer, but it felt good to say the words out loud.

"Tell me I'm doing the right thing," I couldn't help but plead.

As the silence lingered, my heart began beating rapidly. "Rebecca, I'm not ready to do what you asked. It's not right. How could you ask me to do something like that?"

I know my wife loved me. She knows I loved her—still love her. But, anger rose inside me at her final words to me before she died. She'd told me her hopes and dreams for Lilly. She shared her thoughts, hopes, and dreams for me in the future, and that was the part I was having trouble with.

I couldn't help the smile that lifted my lips as I thought about my wife. She was one of the sweetest and most manipulative women I knew. Maybe that's why I loved her so much. She matched me in ways no other woman had.

Even if she hadn't been the one that I'd been initially going after the night we met, I knew everything turned out the way it was supposed to. If I hadn't married Rebecca, there would be no Lilly. Who would have taken care of Rebecca when she was sick? I was the best person for the job.

My life had been good. Amazing.

Who cares if I sometimes wondered what my life would have been like if I'd connected with Norah that night instead of Rebecca? Would she have been good for me? The woman drove me crazy, but she was passionate about what she believed in. No matter what was going on in our lives, she never backed down. She always gave me shit, even when I didn't deserve it.

Even so, she loved fiercely and protected the ones she cared about, which is why she was here now. Yes, I'd demanded that she return and live with us full-time, but I know Norah. She doesn't do anything that she doesn't want to. If she hadn't wanted to be here, she would have stayed in Baltimore. I knew that for a fact.

That didn't help the soul-sucking guilt I felt. How could I look at Norah and think about what a life would have been like if she'd been the one I'd married, when my own wife—her best friend—had only been gone for a year?

Yeah, I'm an asshole.

Chapter 5

Norah

Sitting on my bed in one of the guest rooms of Cade and Rebecca's home, all I wanted to do was cry. Of course, being sad wouldn't help me get through this, but it felt good to put a name on the emotion.

After my confrontation with Cade earlier this morning, I poured everything I could into putting a smile on Lilly's face. We played tag, hide-and-seek, and Go Fish. To keep things balanced, I also made sure she did some pages in the workbook Cade purchased for her. It wasn't going to be all fun and games while I was here, so I might as well start the way I would finish.

My goal with being here was to make sure Lilly was able to have support and stability from the two adults in her life that were still here for her.

Brushing away the tears trailing down my face, I stood from the bed and began to unpack my suitcases. One glance at the clock told me I'd been going for almost sixteen hours straight without sleep. Good thing I took the rest of the week off to get acclimated. Yawning, I shuffled around the room, hanging up clothes in the closet and putting away my underwear and other small clothing into the dresser.

When I told my landlord I would be breaking my lease, I had to pay the early termination fee and decide what to do with my furniture. It had been easier than I thought. Now, I'm living in Cade's home for at least six months to help him raise my goddaughter. When I'd called my mom, she thought I was crazy. At first, she questioned why it had to be me. She didn't understand why I needed to move in when I'd already been visiting them every weekend.

"It's just not right, Norah. I worry about you."

"What do you mean?" I knew what she meant, but I wanted her to say it.

"Honey, I'm not questioning your decision. I'm just wondering if this is the best thing for you. You need your own life. You can't step into someone else's."

Shaking my head, I was disappointed this kept coming up. "Mom, I'm not. I'm Lilly's godmother. I made a promise to Rebecca that I'd look after her daughter if anything ever happened. I'm fulfilling my promise to my best friend."

My mom sighed through the phone. "This has nothing to do with Cade?"

Now I really and truly regretted opening up to my mother all those years ago. At the time, I was sad and upset after a breakup. I'd been thinking about my life and the choices that I made. Then, in a moment of weakness, I told her about how Cade had begun to approach me the night he and Rebecca met. My confession that I'd wanted him for myself had been said in the heat of the moment. Leave it up to my mother to never let me live it down.

"No. Not the way you think. He needs help. All I'm doing is helping."

That call had taken place the day after Cade requested—demanded—that I return. I'd been annoyed that my mother had assumed my intentions were less than honorable. Ha! Listen to me, trying to sound all noble and shit.

Once I was finally done unpacking, I sat on the ottoman at the end of the bed and looked around. The room was nice. A perfect place for me to stay over the next six months. Plus, since Cade had a maid service that came in twice a week, I wouldn't have to do any actual house cleaning. If nothing else, that was a plus.

The room boasted a king-sized bed, cherrywood furniture, and a large bathroom with a separate shower and tub for the occasional soak. The closet was large, and my clothes only fit in half the space. Fine, so sue me. I wasn't really a clothes hound. Put me in comfy leggings, sweats, or maxi dresses, and I was fine. Since I worked from home most days, I didn't have to worry about buying an entire wardrobe of office clothes. If I needed to head to a client meeting, I had what I needed to show up polished and professional.

Removing my baggy shirt, I brushed my teeth and pulled my hair up into a loose bun. Then, just as I was about to pull out my e-reader and settle in with a good book, I heard a small knock, then the door began to open.

"Auntie Norah?"

Putting aside the device, I quickly made my way over to Lilly as she walked into my room. Her face was downcast, and I knew what was happening before she said another word.

"Hey, Lilly Ladybug. What's wrong?"

"I just wanted to make sure you were still here."

And just like that, my heart broke for her all over again. "Yes, sweetheart. I'm here to stay. When you wake up tomorrow, I'm going to be right here. Then the next day and day after that."

"I was scared. Can you read me another story?"

Tilting my head, I tried to come up with a reason why I could send her to bed without giving in, but then, she turned those blue eyes on me, and I was lost. "Yes, come on. One story, and then you have to go to sleep. Tomorrow morning, I'll make us pancakes."

Grabbing my hand, she led me down the hallway to her bedroom. "Thanks, auntie Norah. Daddy always wants to make waffles and eggs. Pancakes are my favorite, but sometimes he doesn't listen."

A smile lifted my lips. Yeah, that sounded like the Cade I knew. Well, maybe the man I always thought he was. If I were honest with myself, he was a lot different than I'd painted him out to be. He was a good man. One who loved his family. A businessman who worked hard every day. I couldn't find fault with him on that.

Maybe my mom was right after all. What-ifs were a horrible thing. Living in the land of what could have been, was no way to live my life. Being here with Cade and Lilly didn't mean I couldn't move on with my life. Of course, any man I dated would have to understand how things were. There was no way I was leaving Lilly. Not before six months anyway. Maybe not even after that.

Once she was in bed and wrapped up in the comforter, I picked up her favorite book full of numerous fairytales. “Which one will it be tonight?”

“Um,” she said with a smile, her little finger tapping against the side of her cheek. “The one with the princess in the tower.”

Nodding, I opened the book to the story. “You got it.”

After ten minutes, Lilly’s eyes were closed, her mouth had fallen open, and she was off in dreamland. No doubt thinking of more ways to make me do what she wanted. Not that she’d have to try very hard. Closing the book, I lifted from the bed. Before I left, I smoothed her blonde hair from her forehead and kissed it. “I love you, Lilly Ladybug.”

I turned on the night light and went to leave but stopped at the sight in front of me.

Cade was standing there in the door, leaning against the doorsill. I almost screamed but caught myself. "How long have you been standing there," I snapped at him as I walked out the room.

"I got up to get some water and noticed the light on in Lilly's room."

We both turned and stepped away. Now that she was asleep, neither of us wanted her to wake up again. Although I hadn't been living here full-time during this past year, I knew how difficult it was for her to go down at night.

As I looked at him, I noticed he stood in front of me in only a pair of red shorts. He was bare up top, and my gaze was drawn to the tattoos covering his chest and arms. To the outside person looking in, Cade looked like a badass biker dude. His dark hair, beard, tattoos, and muscled form made him look dangerous. Not that he wasn't, but from what I understand, he left that life behind him.

According to what I knew about him, he'd joined the US Marine Corps right out of high school. He was one of the guys who carried a gun and went toward the danger when everyone else was running away from it. He'd gotten his bachelor's degree in business management and an MBA before he finished. He was literally the whole package, and here I was standing with him in the hallway of his home while he was half-naked.

"Thank you," he whispered.

Just by looking up at him, I could feel my nipples beading. I crossed my arms and took a step back. I needed to get a fucking grip. Then his words registered. "Why are you thanking me?"

He rubbed a large hand over his short hair. Muscles rippled in his arm, chest, and his abs… all eight of them, flexed with the motion.

"For being here. I know I kind of forced your hand."

Shaking my head to deny his words, I raised my hand to reach out to him, but paused. If I touched him, I knew it would be a bad decision. Yes, he may have pushed the issue, but I wouldn't be here if I didn't want to be. For a moment, I stared into his face and my heart hurt for him and everything he was dealing with. Before I could make a huge mistake, I pulled my hand back, wrapping my arms around my body. Did he see what I'd almost done? From the look of shock on his face, it seemed that he had. My gaze shifted away for a moment, and I took a step back to clear my head. Um… what was I saying? Oh yeah.

"You don't have to thank me. This is what I'm here for, so you don't have to do it alone." For my own sanity, I needed to get back to my bedroom.

"What I said earlier, you know, about you trying to replace Rebecca—"

I truly hoped he wouldn't make it worse and say something stupid that would make me regret being here.

"All I meant was that I know you're not here to replace her. I know that you love Lilly and that you're here to help me with her. It means a lot to me. Your friendship with Rebecca is the one reason you're here, even if it means giving up the life you had in Baltimore. Just, thank you."

This time I looked at him, really looked at him. He looked tired, worn down, and achingly sad. He had every right to be this way, and it made me feel even worse for my feelings for him.

"You're welcome, Cade. Don't worry about Lilly. She's going to be okay. I'm here to help her get through this." And she would be the only person I would focus on. Her father, no matter how sexy he may be, was completely off-limits. “Good night. I’ll see you in the morning. Oh, I’m making pancakes, so don’t be late.” Stepping away from him, I nodded and gave him a slight smile.

Maybe we hadn’t always gotten along in the past, and tonight was not the time to examine why, but it was time to create a new friendship. We could be like roommates. Siblings. Okay, maybe that was too much. If nothing else, we could be friends.

“Good night, Norah.”

Back in my room, I pressed my forehead against the door for a moment before heading over to the bed. Sadness seemed to hover over me like a dark cloak. I wasn’t sure how I would make it over the next six months, but I had to do it somehow. There was no choice.

As I picked up my tablet, I saw that I had some new emails. I noticed there was a response from The Love Vixen, so I clicked the message. My hands shook as I read it:

Dear Virginia,

Oh sweetie, you are in a pickle.

Grief has no timeline and he's still mourning. You need to take a step back and focus on his child while he heals. You are a remarkable woman to rearrange your life in order to be there for the little girl. With patience and compassion, he may one day realize what has been right in front of him.

You asked me what you should do? There isn't an easy answer. Is life ever easy? Listen to your heart. It seems like you already know what to do.

Good luck, hon!

The ♥ Vixen

Well, damn, there it was. Proof that I needed to get over myself. I would have enough on my hands just making sure Lilly was okay. My feelings for Cade would have to go on the backburner. No more wishing for more. No more questioning what my life would be like in an alternate reality.

No more.

Enough.

My love for Lilly would have to be enough to keep me going. It would have to be.

Chapter 6

Cade

Three Months Later

"Where are you going?" Norah was dressed in a yellow sundress, her hair out and curly, and she wore sensible brown leather sandals. Standing in front of me, she chugged the glass of orange juice that I sat in front of her.

"Out," she responded, a smile on her face.

"Smart aleck. That tells me nothing. Where are you going?"

I wanted to know why she was so happy this morning. She'd been heading out more on her own now that we'd found a rhythm that seemed to work for us. Lilly was sleeping more at night. She was back in school, at least until it let out for the summer in a couple weeks, and the smile that I was afraid she'd lost had started to come back.

All in all, life was looking very good.

Because of Norah.

She nibbled on a piece of bacon then leaned up against the counter. I couldn't help but watch her lips move as she ate. Then her tongue peeked out to grab a crumb, and my dick hardened with need.

What the fuck? I didn't want Norah like that. Then again, if that were true, why the hell was I responding to her this way?

She'd been a lifesaver to Lilly and me, stepping in when we needed her the most. During the past three months, it seemed her entire focus was on helping my baby girl get better. They'd spend hours talking about Rebecca, building strong memories that Lilly could keep of her mother. Norah had gone home one weekend to her mother's house in

Alexandria, Virginia. She returned with a box of photos and other mementos from her childhood. Every picture featured Rebecca. They'd spent days going through everything.

Norah had allowed Lilly to pick out several photos that she wanted to keep. They were now framed and plastered all over the walls of her bedroom or sitting on her dresser. Even I could see that Lilly was able to connect with her mother in ways that would never have been possible with only me to take care of it.

Had I needed Norah to move into our home to live with us? At this point, I honestly wasn't sure. What I did know was that I was desperate at the time. After Rebecca passed away and I was on my own, I'd tried everything I could to help my daughter. It was a genius idea to have Norah come to our home. Within three months, things were getting back to some level of normalcy.

The one thing missing from this equation was Rebecca, but even that feeling of loss had lessened some. By the time she'd passed away, we'd said our goodbyes. We'd had time to talk about the things we regretted—my twenties, her hair in high school. She and I spent hours talking about the things we loved—each other, even if I didn't say it every day.

She made me laugh when I wanted to sulk. The day she shaved her head, she cried in my arms for hours, then I told her if it worked for Mike Tyson, it would work for her. She didn't appreciate the comparison but laughed anyway.

My love for my wife was undeniable, but the pain didn't flare up as often as it did before. When I slept in our bed, my dreams weren't filled with visions of her slipping from my grip. It seemed they were now full of her laughter and those moments when she smiled at me in her unique way.

Lately, though, it was almost as if she were trying to speak to me in my dreams. Her lips would move, but I wasn't able to hear her words. No matter how much I tried, I couldn't hear her. The more frustrated I would get, the more she would smile and stroke my face, her fingers tangling in my beard.

I still missed her so damn much, but now I could look back on our life and smile rather than curse fate for giving me a taste of the good life, only to rip it away from me when I was least expecting it.

"Hey, Cade? You still with me?" Norah was calling out to me, her small hand resting on my arm.

She'd been doing that a lot more lately. Asking me if I were okay, touching me lightly to ground me to the present, or simply standing quietly as I worked through whatever emotion I was dealing with. No more challenging me. No more giving me shit. No more getting up in my face.

After that night outside Lilly's bedroom, when Norah had finished reading her the story, something had changed. It wasn't that she was rude or that things were uncomfortable. No, in fact, our living arrangements had become the most stable thing in my life. Part of what made Norah special was her ability to call me out on my bullshit.

Now, things were different. I'm not sure how I felt about it.

"Yeah, I'm still here," I quipped, taking a sip of my coffee. "You still haven't answered my question. Where you headed?"

A soft smile lingered on her lips as she stepped back. Is it crazy that I didn't like her moving away from me? Yeah, that wasn't something I was willing to delve into right now.

"I told you, Cade. I'm headed out with some girlfriends. There's the food truck festival in Old Town Alexandria. We've been planning this for weeks."

Oh yeah, now I remember. She'd offered to take Lilly, but I decided to keep her with me instead. Norah had spent so much time taking care of us, being here for us, that there was no way I was going to have Lilly following behind her on a day meant for Norah and her friends.

"Is that what you're wearing?" I asked. Not that she looked terrible or anything, but that yellow against her skin brought out a glow. Her glorious, thick, natural hair glistened. It didn't look like she was wearing any make-up, but she was beautiful no matter what.

Whoa! Hold your horses, buddy. Stop ogling your late wife's best friend.

She looked down at herself and then looked at me with confusion in her eyes. "Yeah. What's wrong with what I'm wearing? I've been dying to wear this dress for months. It's been sitting in my closet for a while. You don't like it?" She grabbed the fabric near her legs and pulled it wide before twirling around. "I feel like Belle."

Something about seeing her carefree smile made my chest ache. "Then I must be the Beast," I mumbled low under my breath.

Norah stopped turning. "What was that? I couldn't hear you."

Shaking my head, I chose not to repeat myself. "Sit. You need to eat."

"Fine," she said, plopping down in a chair at the marble counter that served as a makeshift dining area. "Why are you always trying to feed me? I think I've gained ten pounds since I moved in. Lord knows I don't need to gain any more weight."

Lifting my gaze to her face, I walked over to her, closing the distance. "Hey." When she looked at me, her brown eyes were wide with questions. "Just... don't talk about yourself like that. You can eat whatever you want, when you want. Plus, I don't see anything wrong with how you look. Any woman should be thankful to have the type of body you do. Okay? And if a man can't appreciate a woman that doesn't look like a stick, then that's their problem." I stared at her for a few seconds as her mouth fell open. Nodding my head, I motioned to her again. "No more of that, okay?"

"Um, yeah. Okay," she said as we stared at each other for another second.

Stepping back over to the stove, I finished up the eggs, potatoes, and bacon. "Is Lilly still up in her room?"

"Yeah, she was brushing her teeth. I laid out some shorts and a shirt for her to put on. She should be down in a few minutes."

More silence as I made a plate for Norah and then for Lilly. It wasn't uncomfortable. There was just nothing to say. Over the past few months, I found that we didn't need to fill the silence with words just to hear ourselves speak. I liked that about Norah. If she had something to say, nothing could stop her. If the situation didn't require her to speak, she was fine staying silent.

"How long will you be gone?" I couldn't help asking her. Not that I would miss her or anything, but I was just curious.

"How long?" She lifted another forkful of eggs to her mouth.

"Yeah. Today. Your little outing. How long will you be gone?" I loved spending time with Lilly, but that didn't mean I couldn't also worry about when Norah would be back. She was living in my house, which meant she was my responsibility. Right?

Wiping her mouth with a napkin, she looked at me with an eyebrow lifted. "Are you worried about me?"

"No, I just—"

Lilly chose that moment to come down the stairs and bounced into the kitchen. "Morning, Daddy. Morning, auntie Norah."

"Morning, honey," I said.

"Hey, ladybug," Norah said with a smile. She lifted Lilly to sit next to her. "Do you remember that I'm going out with friends today?"

I watched the two of them interact and couldn't help but think about how this felt right. It felt good. Logically, I knew something could feel good even if the reason it existed was bad. Watching Norah and Lilly together, I pictured my life one year or even five years from now. This is the scene I wanted to wake up to every morning. I could almost imagine it now. Norah, Lilly, and maybe a little boy who had my eyes and his beautiful momma's smile.

At the vision in my mind, I jerked back.

What the fuck was I thinking?

"Cade? You good?" Norah asked, her eyes on me, a worried frown on her face.

"I'm fine," my tone was short. Judging from the way her eyes squinted and her lips pulled tight, she heard it too. Damn, why'd I have to look at her lips? They were covered in gloss and looked so soft. I wonder what it would feel like to kiss her.

"Why are you so grumpy? I thought you'd be happy to have me out of here for the day. You know, give you a break from me."

She was really pushing me today. "I never said I wanted a break from you. If you never leave outside those doors, that's just fine with me. Don't ever think you need to leave because of me. That's not how this works."

Hell, I never wanted her to leave at all. Even though we both worked and were away from home on occasion, when I got home at the end of a long day, it felt good to walk in and see her waiting for me. Or to walk in and hear her and Lilly laughing. Guilt was a hell of a feeling, but it didn't stop me from seeking her out when I was home.

There was no way I should be feeling this way about Norah. Rebecca had been gone for just over a year. This was too soon. I didn't understand my feelings or why she was the one I pictured by my side in the future. Maybe I was just projecting because I was lonely. It had been almost two years since I'd made love to another woman. One year since I was able to stand around and have a normal conversation without dealing with the effects of cancer ravaging the body of the woman I loved. More than two years since I could simply enjoy a Saturday morning cooking breakfast without thinking about death and grief and fighting the good fight every day.

It felt good.

Which told me I was treading in murky waters. Glancing over at Norah, who was smiling down at Lilly, my heart stuttered. Oh, hell, I'd made the absolute wrong mistake bringing her into our home.

The conversation we had months ago, standing in the hallway, came back to me. No, she wasn't Rebecca. She could never replace my wife. But from everything I was feeling inside right now, that wasn't the problem.

Norah had found a way to make me want to live again. When around her, I smiled more and snapped less. Even at work, my employees seemed more relaxed around me than they'd been in over a year. I was falling for my daughter's godmother, and I had no way to stop it.

Fuck!

What was I going to do now?

Chapter 7

Norah

Walking into the house from my outing, I slid off my sandals and pushed them against the wall. They sat along the wall with multiple pairs of Lilly's shoes and even some of Rebecca's that had never been moved. Cade didn't have any shoes in the living room. For a man like him, that would never be acceptable.

Sighing, I closed my eyes for a moment as I braced myself to see him. It had gotten harder over the past three months, being around him, yet not being able to be who I truly am. Once I'd gotten the response from The Love Vixen, I knew I had to get a grip. My schoolgirl crush on Cade wasn't very helpful.

It didn't matter that my stomach clenched in need whenever he got close to me.

Whenever we were in the kitchen, and he walked close to me, his cologne in the air, the heat of his body, would turn something on inside me. The man hardly ever touched me, other than maybe a hand on my arm to get my attention for something Lilly did. Nothing about our interactions could be seen as anything other than friendly, platonic, and boring.

There were moments when it was just the two of us alone at the end of the day, when it felt right just being here. We'd be in the family room while the television played. I'd be watching a show, feet tucked up underneath me. Cade would be sitting in the wingback chair, working on his laptop. Occasionally, he'd grunt or murmur in response to something happening on the show.

It was comfortable. It was how we ended most nights unless he stayed out late for client meetings or one of us had to travel. It was a good life. A stable life. But maybe it wasn't my life to live.

Three months were left in our agreement, but honestly, I didn't know how I would handle being in his presence that long. I was hanging on by a thread, and it was getting thinner every day.

Take this morning when he asked me about where I was going. It took everything in me to leave the house. I was trying more and more to build a life outside of being there for Cade and Lilly. It had gotten so bad for me, that I was now starting to make up things to do just so I could leave. Yeah, it was somewhat childish, but what else was I going to do?

The longer I stayed, the more I wanted.

"Why are you just standing there?"

I jumped at his voice. "Damnit, Cade!"

He raised one eyebrow at me. "Why are you yelling at me? You're the one standing by the door like a statue." He held a glass in his hand. Brown liquor filled the bottom as he took a sip. "Where have you been all day? I thought you'd be back home earlier than this."

Home…that word still shocked me. Was this my home? I glanced around at the little things I'd done to put my stamp on things. It wasn't my home, but it was where I lay my head at night. It was where the two most important people in the world lived.

"I called you a couple of times, but you didn't pick up."

Shaking my head to clear away the fog, I followed behind him when he turned and walked into the family room. "You called me?"

"Why didn't you pick up?"

Damn, this man had a one-track mind. "I was busy." I'd seen when those calls had come through, but simply chose not to pick up. Cade usually called at least once when I was out for the day. Usually, it was something mundane, but I had a feeling that he expected me to pick up when he called. No matter what I was doing, he knew I would answer when he needed me. So, today I decided to take a different approach. I wanted him to see that I wasn't always at his beck and call.

"Norah? You keep zoning out. What's going on with you lately?"

If only he knew. Watching him sit down on the couch, I knew we were in for a long night. His spot was the wingback chair. My spot was the couch. Staring at him, I shrugged my shoulders before walking to the other side of the couch and sitting next to him. Lifting my bare feet, I placed them on the table in front of us. I laid my head against the back cushion of the couch, and I sighed.

"Nothing's wrong with me. I just had a day for myself. Whatever you needed couldn't have been that important."

He placed his drink down, then he half-turned to glare at me. "How do you know? You didn't even have the decency to pick up when I called. What if something was wrong with Lilly?"

"Cade. We have codes, remember? It was what you asked for. If something was wrong with Lilly, you would text me the code you established when I first got here. Unless you've forgotten your own rules, which you would never do, I know for a fact nothing was wrong with Lilly."

His nostrils flared as he breathed in and out. Those gorgeous lips of his thinned, and his green eyes stared at me as if he wanted to say more. After a few more seconds, he huffed, stood, and walked over to his chair. He didn't sit down. Looking at his back, it was like he took a deep breath before turning to face me.

"When I call, you answer. No matter what you're doing or who you're with," he snapped.

I wanted to laugh at the fucking audacity. "No. It doesn't work that way. If there's an emergency, then put in the damn code. If you're calling me about finding a barrette for her hair, then deal with it yourself. When I'm out—with someone—then I'm on my own time. I don't answer to you."

He shook his head. "How could you have been best friends with Rebecca? You're so damn different. I can't understand how she put up with your attitude for so long. Every word out of your mouth is a fucking challenge. You don't know how to get along with anyone. I thought I was bad, but you just walk through life as if no one matters but you. You are here for me… and Lilly. You're here to help Lilly. As her father, when I reach out to you, then it's always something to do with her." He briefly closed his eyes before staring down at me again. "When I call, you fucking pick up."

As he continued fussing at me about answering my phone, I was still stuck on his words about my friendship with Rebecca. Our friendship was something that lasted our entire lives. Our differences are what made us perfect. She was the yin to my yang. She was sweet and I was sour. She was the lightning, and I was the thunder.

"Fuck you, Cade."

"What?"

Standing from the couch, I rushed over to stand in front of him. "I said, fuck you. You don't get to question my friendship with Rebecca. You don't get to take out your bullshit on me. You don't know anything about me."

"Why would I want to?" Harsh words from a cruel man.

Didn't he realize everything I did, every day of my life since Rebecca had died, had been for him and Lilly?

"You're an asshole," I yelled at him.

"That's what others have told me."

My anger burned hot. I'd only left today because I needed him to focus on spending time with his daughter. Every day, we spent time as this family unit, but it was all wrong. It made me feel raw. I thought that I'd stepped into a life that didn't fit me. Looking at the man who filled my dreams at night, the one man who could heat up my body with just a look, I regretted the day I met him. I wished he had never entered my orbit. Maybe then I wouldn't want him so much.

"Why did Rebecca even marry you? Maybe if you hadn't married her, my friend would still be alive."

As soon as the words left my mouth, I regretted them. That wasn't fair to Cade. It wasn't his fault that Rebecca was gone. Once she was diagnosed, he'd done everything in his power to get her better. The best doctors. The best nurses. No matter how hard it was, he was right by her side.

"I'm sorry!"

He took a step back as if I'd landed a physical blow. "Is that what you really think? That being with me killed Rebecca?" His body was stiff and his words were rough.

Shaking my head, I reached out one hand to touch him. He pulled back, as if repulsed. "Cade. I'm sorry."

"No. Don't apologize now. You said what you felt. Now I know this is how you feel about me. You blame me for Rebecca's death. Is that why you leave sometimes? Is that why you don't answer my calls?"

I could feel the tears welling in my eyes. "No, that's not what I feel at all. It was just... hell, I don't even know what I felt. But I shouldn't have said what I did. I know how much you loved her."

He didn't speak for a few seconds before he stepped around me and began to walk out of the room.

"Where are you going?" It was now my time to ask.

"I think I'm going to sit outside tonight. I need some fresh air."

Now he was the one trying to get away from me. My mom always told me that I was too impulsive. That saying everything on my mind, without using an internal filter, would get me in trouble one day. My temper flamed hot and went cold even quicker.

Looking around, I realized Lilly wasn't hovering around or peeking down at us from the stairs as we yelled at each other. "Where's Lilly?"

He rubbed a hand down his face. "That's what I was calling you about. She spent the night at her friend Jamie's house. We couldn't find her pink blanket with the unicorns."

My eyes widened. "The one Rebecca bought for her?"

Cade nodded. "Yeah, that one. She wanted it for tonight, for her first sleepover. We searched the entire house for it. It wasn't my intention to interfere with your day, but we both thought you would know where it was. But you ignored every message. I finally found it under her bed. Crisis averted."

At his words, I nodded. Not responding or returning his call had backfired. "Damn, Cade. I didn't realize… I didn't think…."

"That's the problem, you didn't think. You blame me for Rebecca dying, and I can accept that. Hell, I blame myself for not doing more. Not noticing something was wrong. But, right here, right now, you're the closest thing to a mother that Lilly has. She depends on you to be there for her. Even in her five-year-old mind, she knows that having you here is a replacement for her mother. Norah, you agreed that you'd be here for her. For us. I know you need your own life—"

"This is my life. Here with Lilly." I wanted to add that my life was with him, but wisely held my tongue. This was so not the time to open that big ass can of worms.

Cade nodded at my interruption, then he snapped. "Then act like it. Stop going off and ignoring my calls. Stop acting as if you're the fucking babysitter. For three months, you've walked around here as if you're a fucking visitor. If you want to be here for Lilly, then be here. Stop hiding. Stop running. Be the mother she needs."

I couldn't help my outburst. "But I'm not her mother. Rebecca is dead!"

Lifting his eyes to the sky, it was as if he prayed for divine intervention. "You don't think I know that? I sleep in a room every night that has her scent, her clothes, those silly romance books she couldn't help but read. I know she's dead. But her daughter is alive. Do you hear me? Lilly is alive. It's bad enough that her mother, my wife, died. But I sure as shit don't want to live in a house with a woman who walks around like she's an invisible guest. A zombie. So, as I said. When I call, you pick up the fucking phone."

After he chewed me a new ass, Cade walked through the house and exited the door leading to the back of the house.

"Fuck!"

My head fell into my hands, and I couldn't help the tears flowing from the well of my eyes. I thought I was over feeling this way.

Guilty.

He was right. I was trying to escape him, this home, and this life, but not for the reasons he thought. It was space from him and the feelings I had. If I didn't separate myself occasionally, it would only get worse. When I spoke to my mom the other day, she asked me if I was doing okay. At first, I thought she was asking about Rebecca. But she clarified that she was asking about how I was doing living with Cade. I'd almost confessed everything to her. My feelings for him—that it was difficult living in the same house while hiding my emotions. That I dreamed of him at night. Visions would play in my mind of his head between my legs, bringing me pleasure as I screamed his name. Or his beard rubbing along my thighs as he lapped up my essence.

Guilty.

Yes, I was guilty of wanting him and it was eating me up inside.

Glancing toward the back of the house, I made a move to go talk to Cade, but decided to leave it alone. We'd said some harsh things to each other. I, for one, was not ready for another round. All I needed to do was say the wrong thing. Well, that had already happened. Just my luck, I'd say something even worse.

Turning to the stairs, I decided to go change. At the silence around me, I realized this was the first time Cade and I had been alone since I'd moved in three months ago.

Yup. I definitely should have answered the phone earlier.

Chapter 8

Norah

I removed my dress and put on some shorts and a graphic t-shirt— typical attire when I finished my day. If I didn't have in-person or video meetings, this was my work attire. I was all about living a comfortable life. Wearing a suit or dressing up every day just wasn't something I wanted. That's one of the reasons I gravitated to doing HR consulting. My expertise didn't require me to wear 3-inch heels and makeup every day.

Once changed, I sat on the end of the bed and thought about the argument I'd just had with Cade downstairs. Was he right? Had I been doing only the bare minimum since I'd moved in? Thinking back on my time here, I could admit that he was right. My focus was supposed to be on helping Lilly, but I also had kept my distance from her. What if she came to rely on me and something happened?

Was I expected to play the role of her replacement mother my entire life?

I was being selfish, and I hated myself for it.

When I agreed to be her godmother, that's what I signed up for. So, what was stopping me from going all in?

Cade.

Just picturing him in my head caused my insides to flutter. He wasn't the type of man who would stay single for the rest of his life. There was no way that women wouldn't gravitate towards him. He was six feet, three inches of sexy goodness and had a body like a god, with tattoos to match. The man was still rough around the edges, no matter how much money was in his bank account or how many custom-made suits he owned. His voice was low and deep, smooth like a good-aged whiskey. And that walk... I couldn't take my eyes from him, whether he was coming or going.

There was something about him that called to me. It had from the very first moment we'd met. Well, the night he met Rebecca. I couldn't help but sigh at the direction my thoughts had taken.

"Forgive me, Rebecca."

There was no answer. How could there be?

"How do I stop feeling this way?"

Again, silence.

Now I felt like I was losing my damn mind. Was I expecting her ghost to somehow show up and tell me it was okay to lust after her husband?

"Girl, you're losing it," I spoke into the silent room.

Those words sounded exactly like something Rebecca would say. I laughed at the thought of her sitting here with me, telling me how I needed to get over myself. She was always the one who could make me smile, even when I didn't want to.

2 Years Ago

Rebecca and I were both lying in bed as we tried to watch a movie. I'd basically been down here for two weeks straight to help her as she went through treatments, which weren't working at all.

It seemed like she was getting worse every day. It hurt to see my friend suffering this way, especially when I could do nothing to help her.

"Norah," she said suddenly. I took my eyes off the TV screen and looked at her. "I know that things aren't looking good. These

doctors are trying to keep our hopes up for me to get better, but I can feel it inside. I don't have much longer."

I shook my head, still in denial. "Yes, you do. You're one of the strongest people I know. We're supposed to grow old together, sitting on our front porch while our husbands watch football, and our kids are off traveling the world. You still have to convince Cade to send us to Paris for the springtime."

"And we'll traipse all over the city and visit the museums and eat pastries all day."

Nodding, I patted her hand. "See, we have things to do. Plans we've made. But wait, what about Lilly?"

Rebecca laughed, "Oh, she'll be here with Cade." At my groan, she continued. "I know he seems like a grumpy bear, but he's good to me. To Lilly." Just then, a coughing fit overcame her. I grabbed some water for her to drink. After a few moments, she continued. "I want you to have that kind of love, Norah."

"I'm fine," I denied quickly. With my luck, I'd never have what Rebecca had. Sometimes, I didn't think I deserved it.

"Stop that," she said, "One day, you're going to get the happiness you deserve. Too bad, I won't be here to see it."

"Stop that, Rebecca."

Rebecca's chest rose and fell as her wheezing became worse. "Just promise me, Norah. If they can't have me, I need them to have you. If things had gone differently years ago, you would—"

"Everything okay?" Cade's deep voice interrupted. "I heard you coughing," he said to his wife.

I wondered what Rebecca had been about to say, but I moved on from that thought when she spoke to Cade standing in the door like a guardian angel. There was a smile hovering on Rebecca's lips as she looked at him.

"Hey, sweetheart. I'm fine. Just talking about the future."

I watched a smile come over his face, but it didn't reach his eyes. Maybe I was the only one who hadn't accepted what was happening.

"That's good, baby. Hey, Lilly wants to come in and hangout with you two. Do you feel up to it?"

Rebecca nodded and shifted her body to sit up a bit straighter. "Of course. I'm always up for a visit from our Ladybug," she said as Lilly squeezed past her father's legs and ran over to the bed.

I glanced up at Cade. For a brief moment, I saw the raw emotion on his face as he watched his wife and daughter. Rebecca may want me to move on and have a life, maybe find someone to love, but she didn't understand what she was saying. Sure, I'd dated over the years and felt deeply for some of them, but they were all missing something. That spark. The sizzle. The only man to ever make me feel that way was off-limits.

My best friend was gone. But I was still here living. I would miss her until my last breath, but Cade was right. I was here for Lilly. To help her grow. To give her all the love I had for my best friend.

For so long, I felt like I'd been in that casket with Rebecca. Felt like I was unworthy of having a life and enjoying myself because she was gone. But I now realize that's not what she would have wanted. It's not what I wanted either.

Lilly was sleeping over at a friend's house tonight, and that was a good thing. It would give me time to get my head right. Cade had a point. My attitude needed an adjustment. No more doing things half-way.

Standing from the bed, I grabbed my phone and walked out of my bedroom. Once I was back downstairs, I looked toward the back of the house and noticed that Cade was still sitting outside.

The first thing I needed to do was apologize. I would hate it, because I'm sure Cade would never let me forget it, but it was something that had to be done. I grabbed a beer from the fridge and took a deep breath to gather my strength. Knowing this moment was long overdue, I walked out the back door and made my way to Cade.

Stepping up to the side of his chair, I looked down at him. His eyes seemed unfocused as he stared out across the large expanse of the backyard.

"I sometimes feel that I don't have the right to be here."

He didn't respond other than to pick up his glass and take a sip of his drink.

"If I don't get too close to you and Lilly, I won't be heartbroken when I need to leave."

The one hand resting on his thigh clenched tight. "Why would you need to leave?"

Now this was a moment of truth. Should she tell him the real reason she felt that way, or should she lie? "One day, you'll move on. You... Lilly, won't need me anymore. Then what happens?" Okay, maybe a half-truth.

His lips thinned and he finally looked up at me. Those green eyes of his were challenging and full of... something. "Lilly will always need you. I..." he cleared his throat. "No one will ever take your place." He took another sip. "Are you finally finished running?"

Slowly, I sat down in the chair next to him, unsure how to answer his question. Would it be a lie if I said I was?

He sighed and said, "Listen, I know what I said earlier, questioning why the two of you were friends hurt you. That wasn't my intention."

"Then what were your intentions? It seemed like you were pretty sure of what you wanted to say to me."

Glancing over at me, his gaze held me frozen. "Rebecca left something for you. A letter that was recently delivered. I was supposed to give it to you when I felt you were fully onboard with helping me raise Lilly. Are you fully onboard?"

What? "A letter? For me? Why didn't you tell me?"

"Did you hear nothing I said just now? It just arrived and Rebecca left it up to me to decide when you were ready. Her only request was that I wait until you were truly accepting of your new role with Lilly. Up until now, I wasn't sure if you were there. But with everything that's happening, I think you are."

I stood. “Of course, I am. Give me the letter right now. Where is it?”

“In my study. Stay here. I’ll go grab it.”

A few minutes later, he returned, a sealed envelope in his hand. Snatching it out of his hand, I wanted to curse his ass out for keeping this from me. Instead, I took a few deep breaths. It wasn’t his fault my friend had a flair for the dramatic.

“You didn’t open it?”

Cade shook his head. “No. It wasn’t my letter. I have my own that was delivered the same day. Your letter was included in the package. Since it was sealed and meant for you, I felt it best to keep it that way.”

“You have a letter, too? Well, what did yours say?”

He paused, staring at me for a few extra seconds. “My letter was for me. Not you. You have your own letter in your hands. Worry about that. I’ll be inside if you want to talk.”

Turning on his heel, he walked away, shutting the patio door behind him. I immediately opened the envelope and pulled out the letter. Rebecca's handwriting jumped out at me, and I smiled. That woman definitely knew how to be unforgettable. Starting at the top, I began reading...

Hey Girl...

Chapter 9

Cade

Walking away from Norah was difficult. My control was slipping. My arms ached to wrap around her, protecting her from the hurt she was about to experience. I know what it feels like to get a letter from the grave. When my letter arrived a few days ago, I stared at it for hours before opening it up. The scent of her perfume was on the pages, and I became angry at fate for taking her away from me. From us.

I rubbed a hand down my face before glancing towards the back of the house. I could see Norah reading the letter. A part of me wished I had opened it to see what she'd said to her friend, but I knew that would have been crossing a line. Norah needed this, just as I did.

I've read Rebecca's letter to me so many times, I could recite it from memory.

My dear Cade,

How long did it take you to open this letter? How long did you stare at it before opening the envelope? I bet you're wondering how I know. Well, it's because I know you. You've been my life partner for eight years. You made my life so magical. From the moment I saw you, you took my breath away.

Thank you for loving me. Thank you for my daughter. Thank you for being such an amazing husband. The man I needed. You made me feel whole.

I know you're holding on to me when you should be letting me go. We knew the day would come when I wouldn't be with you and Lilly. We talked about it. Planned for it. You're a very stubborn man, but even you can't beat death. All those times you held me in your arms, we had our moments to say goodbye.

I know you love me. I've never doubted that.

But I also know that your life could have been different. I didn't realize until later that you'd been walking towards Norah that night. She was the one who caught your eye. Not me. I was ignorant that night, but I couldn't give you up even after realizing the truth.

Did that make me selfish? Probably.

Do I regret it? Not one bit.

I have no doubt that had I lived, we would continue to live our lives loving each other until the very end. But I'm not with you anymore. I can't be, no matter how much I want to be. Sweetheart, it's okay to let me go. It's okay to move on. I want you to focus on the life you can have now that I'm no longer around. No longer in the way.

Norah will be there for you and Lilly, but it's going to take her some time. She would kill me for telling you this, but I see the way she looks at you. And yes, I've even seen the way you look at her. I know there was nothing between you two, but I also have to be realistic about what the future holds.

Don't hold on to a dead woman. There's a living woman right in front of your eyes that if you let yourself live again, you'll find that she's the one for you. Norah is the one you need to make you happy. And, Cade, I want you to be happy. I want you to smile again. I want you to know that you are so deeply loved. That's my wish for you.

Please make sure to tell my little Ladybug that I love her so much. Let down your guard and play with your daughter when she wants to play dress-up or have a tea party. Take her on trips so she can see the world. But most of all, be the dad she needs and help make all her dreams come true.

I love you, Cade. I have always loved you and I know that you love me in return. I want you to live, and I want you to be happy. Just open your eyes to what's right in front of you.

Your 1st wife, Rebecca.

If I had this letter earlier, maybe I wouldn't have felt so guilty about how much I want to be with Norah. A smile lifted my lips as I thought about everything that happened over the past fifteen months. Even in death, Rebecca knew what I needed.

I still couldn't believe what she'd written in that letter. In disbelief, I read it every day, multiple times a day. The words made no sense. Well, some of them did. I was glad to read that she'd been happy. Not that I'd questioned if we had a good life, but my heart clenched when I read it in her own words.

I hadn't always thought that the life I had with Rebecca was within my grasp. In my teenage years, I'd given my parents hell. There was something inside me that rebelled at the good. When I joined the US Marines right out of high school, I viewed it as a way to get my head on straight. I spent eight years being a killing machine and I loved every minute of it. Until I got shot while on a mission, that was when I knew it was time for me to change.

After that, I couldn't see myself living a normal life. Being a husband, father, with 2.5 kids, and a white picket fence. People like me didn't get to have a good life. I was meant to suffer because my sins were too many to count.

Then I went out for a drink one night.

I saw a woman across the room and my entire world changed. Her smile beckoned me closer. Her eyes captured mine and I wanted to know how she looked in the morning when she first woke up. My fingers itched to touch her skin to see if it was as soft as it looked. Everything inside me responded to her. Then she looked away for a moment. The next second, another woman approached.

I thought I'd lost my moment. She walked away and when I tried to follow her, the blonde grabbed my hand.

Even as I sat and talked with the other woman, who was beautiful in her own right, I wondered where the other woman had gone. That answer came fifteen minutes later when she approached us. Looking down at the blonde's hand on my leg and my arm resting on the back of her chair, she plastered a smile on her face.

Then Rebecca introduced us. "Hey, Norah. Where were you? This is Cade," she said, motioning to me. "Cade, this is my best friend, Norah."

When her brown eyes met mine, I felt my heart stop beating in my chest. It was her. The woman I'd been approaching when Rebecca stopped me. Just my fucking luck. I could feel my hands become sweaty as I sat there staring at her. "Hi Norah. Nice to meet you." Stupid words but they were expected.

When she'd turned to me, all I wanted to do was shift away from Rebecca and make my interest known. Something in Norah's eyes stopped me, holding me in place. "Cade, is it?" At my nod, she continued. "Nice to meet you as well." She looked at Rebecca and smiled. "Well, it's a good thing I left. Seems like you've been busy." Then she ignored me for the rest of the night.

The moment had been so fleeting. It was like I'd been struck by lightning. My entire world had been focused on Norah, until it wasn't.

Over the years, I thought I'd hidden my attraction to Norah. She wasn't the one I fell in love with, she wasn't the one I married, or who had my child. Rebecca had been a good wife to me, and I'd been a good husband to her. But that doesn't mean sometimes, when I'm alone in that big bed, knowing that Norah was right down the hallway, that I didn't think about what would have happened if I hadn't allowed Rebecca to stop me that night. What if I kept going after Norah? What type of life would I have? Would I be happy?

Just the thought of a different life with Norah was almost too much to bear. There was no going back. The past could not be changed, but does that mean I couldn't change my future?

Does she even think of me that way? I know Rebecca's letter said she saw the way Norah looked at me, but that could have been imagined. We could hardly be in the same room without arguing with each other. I know my reasons, but what were hers? She'd never given any indication that she was attracted to me. Hell, she's been living in my home for three months, and even before that, she was with us every weekend for an entire year.

If she felt something, anything, wouldn't I have seen it already?

I know I was attractive, so that wasn't the issue. Before Rebecca, my entire focus had been on having as many women as I could. Commitment was a bad word to me. Being connected to just one woman wasn't something I wanted for myself. Playing the field was what I preferred, until Rebecca made an honest man out of me. Even now, once word got out that my wife had passed, women seemed to be coming out of the woodworks. I had no interest in any of them. My dick wouldn't even get hard for them.

But it reacted to Norah. It had been doing that for months now. She'd walk into the room in leggings and a baggy shirt, and I couldn't take my eyes off her. We'd be sitting in the family room, she'd be wearing shorts and a tank top, and it would take everything in me not to grab her up and fuck her right on the couch.

Those were the feelings coursing through me every time I looked at her.

We were building a life together, even if both of us were reluctant participants. Now that we'd been forced to adapt to each other, stop fighting, and live under the same roof, proximity had shown me that there was more to this life than grief.

Thinking about Rebecca's letter, I sighed in defeat. Was she really giving me permission to move on, with Norah of all people?

Did I want to see where things would go between the two of us?

There was nothing I wanted more.

Glancing up, I looked back at the door to the backyard as Norah walked inside. Her steps were tentative and slow. The envelope was pressed close to her chest and Norah's eyes were downcast. Her look wasn't giving me much, but I figured Rebecca dropped some bombshells in the letter to her best friend as well.

"Norah? You okay?" I couldn't help but ask as she walked inside as if in a trance.

Lifting her head, she stared at me with glistening eyes. Nodding, she folded the letter and placed it in the pocket of her shorts. "Um, I'm fine."

"Did you read the letter?" I wanted to know what Rebecca had said to her but knew I didn't have that right. When she'd asked me about my letter, I told her it was private. It would be foolish of me to demand she share the contents of her letter with me. I wanted to know what it said, but I'd have to depend on her to tell me willingly.

She looked off to the side before glancing at me again. "I did."

"Did she share the secrets of the universe with you?"

Norah was looking shell-shocked and out of pocket. This wasn't like her at all. This shit was starting to worry me.

Pouring her beer in the sink, she threw the bottle away, and came in my direction. Why did anticipation flare-up inside me? What was I expecting her to do?

Norah smiled. "No secrets of the universe. But she had a wicked sense of humor. Then again, she'd always been that way." She stepped around him. "Hey, I'm gonna go up to bed. I just need to lie down."

Now I was worried. "Are you sure you're okay? Anything I can do to help? You know I'm here for you, right?" Her eyes got wide at my words, and I had an eerie feeling that I knew precisely what Rebecca had placed in that letter.

"Thanks, Cade, but I'm okay. Just a bit of a headache. I'll see you in the morning."

"Okay. 'Night, Norah."

"Goodnight, Cade."

As she walked away, why did I get the feeling I was missing something? Was this one of those moments that would define my future? My mouth moved but no words came out. Even if Norah's letter did say what I think it did, she was just now processing it. Now wasn't the time for me to say anything. Then again, when was the right time?

Chapter 10

Norah

Shock.

Yes, that had to be it. I was in a state of shock. I couldn't even cry because my brain was too busy going over the letter left for me by my best friend—a literal letter from the grave. Rebecca always did have a morbid sense of humor.

Slowly climbing the stairs, I could feel Cade's gaze on my back as I walked away. It was like a laser beam was focused on me, searing my skin, my soul. Today had been the craziest damn day. Maybe I was dreaming. Yeah, that had to be it.

"Ouch!" Okay, so pinching myself wasn't the wisest decision but it did mean I wasn't asleep. Which meant, that crazy ass letter really did exist. I glanced down at my hands with the envelope still in my grasp.

Finally making it to my bedroom, I closed the door and sat down on the bed. So many thoughts going through my head. Pulling out the letter, I read it one more time. And the shock and surprise were still there with every single word.

Hey Girl,

Listen, don't freak out. Just read all the way through and if you want to curse me out after that, feel free. I don't think you will though.

Norah, you are my best friend. We've known each other since we both wore pigtails and thought boys had cooties. Actually, they still have cooties, but now their cooties come with muscles and sexy smiles and big... egos. Come on, you know that's funny.

You are the only person who knows my secrets, even the ones I'm ashamed of, like that time in ninth grade with Bobby Jones. I still can't believe I was that stupid. But even with every mistake, every tear, every laugh, we never stopped being there for each other. When my dad died, you were my shadow The only person who could get me to eat, bathe (yeah, I was a skunk), and start to live again.

You are my sister, my best friend, and the only person I could see in Lilly's life to help her grow. I know you thought being a godmother would only involve unique gifts on birthdays, international trips as she got older, and giving her a safe space when Cade and I pissed her off. I know this is not what you expected.

Surprise!

It's going to be okay, Norah. I may not physically be with you, but I will always be around. In the memories we share, the look on

Lilly's face when you make her laugh, and the love you have for my little girl. So, thank you. Thank you for being there for her. Thank you for being my best friend.

Now, to the real reason you're reading this. I want you to stop mourning me. No, that does not mean you have to stop missing my smile or my fantastic dance moves. But depending on when Cade gives you this letter, it means you've been living a half-life, still waiting on me to return. I'm not. You must move forward because I don't want you to stop living or having fun or laughing that crazy snort-laugh thing you do.

Your goddaughter needs you to show her what the world is like in full color, and I have a feeling you're not doing that. So, I say this with so much love... Cut the shit, chick.

And most importantly, I want you to open yourself to love. None of those guys were right for you and I'm glad you didn't fall into the trap of marrying one of them. The man meant for you is closer than you think.

Norah, I know why you didn't come to the house and visit as often as I wanted. I know it was difficult seeing me with Cade. If that night we both met him had gone differently, then I have no doubt you would be with him. Don't worry. I know the two of you never did anything. I'm confident in his feelings for me.

When did I know? How did I know? A few months after he and I started dating, I was already half in love with him. We talked about that first night and I realized you'd seen him first, that he was moving in your direction. At the time, I'd been blind to anything but him and so I moved in first. Not realizing you'd caught his eye.

If I'd known, I'd never have approached him. But I did, and you know the rest.

Cade is an amazing husband and an even better father. If you got to know him, you'd see it too. Now that I'm finally out of the way (Kidding! I'm kidding!). Seriously, I want you to know that you're the only woman I'd ever do this with, but I want you to give Cade a chance. I want you to think of him as you would any other man, not the husband of your dead best friend. Whew! I guess it's time I get used to saying that.

Stop running away. He needs you. Lilly needs you. And if you can finally admit it, you need them too.

Now, don't be all weird the next time you see him. Act normal and don't be all shifty like you usually are. I want you to be happy. I want you to have the kind of love I've had for so long. I know it may be eight years too late, but you and Cade have the rest of your lives to make up for lost time. Don't waste it!

Never forget. I love you. You're my sister, my best friend. Now, go live the life you were meant to live.

Your sister from another mister, Rebecca

The letter dropped from my hand and fell to the floor. My eyes filled with tears, but I refused to let them fall. I could not believe her words, even if I'd read them with my own eyes. Even though she was gone, Rebecca was still bossy as ever. What was wrong with her?

Laughter rumbled through my chest until I couldn't help the sound from escaping my mouth. Did my best friend just give me permission to go after her husband? No fucking way? Why would she do that?

"Ouch! Damn!" Okay, I needed to stop pinching myself because I was clearly still awake. If I was awake, then there had to be another excuse for what was happening. The Twilight Zone© had to be a real thing because shit like this didn't happen in real life.

Maybe I should be more worried that Rebecca knew I had a thing for her husband. Not that I would have ever done anything to hurt her, which is why I stayed away. Based on her letter, my efforts weren't fooling anyone. At least not Rebecca anyway. I had to wonder why she wasn't more upset. Leaning down, I picked up the letter again and skimmed the content.

In the back of my mind, I'd always wondered if she knew Cade had seen me first. Had that been the reason why she'd intercepted him?

8 Years Ago

"Hey, I'm gonna go grab a drink. Want something?"

Looking at Rebecca, I shook my head. "No. I'm good for now," I said, lifting my half-filled glass.

"Okay, I'll be back." As Rebecca walked away, men's heads turned in her direction.

I couldn't help but shake my head. My friend had no idea just how attractive she was. She was clueless to just how much attention she got whenever we went out. She often said the same thing about me. We both knew we looked damn good; her pale skin, blonde hair, and blue eyes to my brown skin, black hair, and brown eyes. We were the opposite in so many ways. She was sweet as pie, even if she was a bit bossy. I was sour, but inside I was filled with all the soft mushy stuff not many people had a chance to experience.

Glancing around the space, I watched people with their heads down, whispering and smiling. I wasn't sure if they'd met tonight or were couples when they arrived. One day, that would be me. I'd find my prince charming, and he'd treat me like the queen I am. Maybe not tonight, but it would be soon. I was fine with waiting for the right man.

Just then, my eyes stopped on a man standing across the room.

Damn, he was fine. Dark hair. Close-cut beard. He was wearing that black suit as if it had been made just for him and maybe it had been. His eyes captured mine across the crowded space and I felt my core clench.

Predator.

My brain short-circuited. A frisson of electricity ran along my skin. The hair on my arms raised. My breath caught in my throat. I heard a low moan and realized it was me. I wanted to run my fingers along his short hair, through his beard. Was it as soft as it looked? Was his body as hard as it appeared underneath his suit. I couldn't take my eyes from him and from the look he gave me, he knew it.

He smirked at me. I smiled at him.

It wasn't that I came out tonight with the intentions of meeting a man, but I was open to whatever the night would bring. I'd been single for more than two years and it was lonely. Sure, I could have hooked up with guys during that time, but I was tired of playing the games. Waking up in my bed alone after the guy left in the middle of the night wasn't something I wanted to experience again. It happened once and that was enough for me.

But, for the man standing across the room staring at me like I was a tasty treat, I would be willing to risk it.

It was as if time stood still. Then he moved toward me, and everything came crashing back. The noise from the people surrounding us. The crush of the crowd. I shifted to the side, moved out of someone's way. He kept walking, moving in my direction, his gaze on me as if I were his prey. Funny thing was, I wanted to be caught.

"Excuse me," someone said, bumping into me.

Shifting again, I stepped to the side, moving out of their way. Then a group of people walked in front of me, and I took another step back. Finally getting my bearing, I looked up to find the man who'd been making his way toward me and couldn't find him. Looking around, I noticed that I was a few feet away from where I'd been standing. There must have been a wave of people who'd come inside, and I swear every single one of them stood in front of me.

"Fuck," I said under my breath. "Really?" Disappointment coursed through me. He was gone. I'd lost the chance. Maybe if I get lucky, I'll meet him again, but the moment was gone. "Unbelievable. Just my fucking luck," I murmured. Sitting my drink down, I walked out of the crowded space. Time for a bathroom break and to get some fresh air.

Fifteen minutes later, I made my way back into the crowded bar area and made my way across the room. I spotted Rebecca's blonde hair and the silver shimmery dress among the crowd. Thankfully, she found a seat. Good, because my damn feet hurt, and I need to sit down. The closer I got to her, the slower my steps became. She was sitting with someone. A man wearing a black suit. Dark hair.

This was not happening.

When they both turned my way, my stomach dropped.

Yes, it was.

The man who'd been looking at me. The only man who'd captured my attention in months. Yeah, he was sitting with my best friend, and they looked mighty damn cozy.

Fuck my life.

Then Rebecca introduced us. "Hey, Norah. Where were you? This is Cade," she said, motioning at the man sitting there looking at me with shock in his eyes. "Cade, this is my best friend, Norah."

When my eyes met his, I felt my heart stop beating in my chest. It was him. I could feel my hands become sweaty as I stood there staring at the two of them sitting together. Did my heart crack a little? Yeah, it sure as hell did. Did regret fill my body that Rebecca was sitting with him and not me? Absolutely.

"Hi, Norah. Nice to meet you." His voice was like warm molasses. Smooth. Smoky. Deep.

Whatever I'd thought when I first saw him, shifted. Even if I wanted him, it was too late. "Cade, is it?" He nodded. "Nice to meet you as well." Glancing over at Rebecca, I plastered a smile on my face. "Well, it's a good thing I stepped out. Seems like you've been busy."

Then I did the only thing I could to keep my sanity. I ignored Cade for the rest of the night.

Sitting here, I couldn't stop the laughter. At this point, it was a bit hysterical, filled with disbelief. Yet, still, I wondered just what the hell was I going to do now?

Chapter 11

Cade

Less than thirty minutes after Norah went upstairs, I followed. The house was silent, and I was tired. It had been a long day and an even longer night. I'd spent the last fifteen minutes questioning if giving her the letter tonight was the right thing to do.

Norah thought I didn't know she was running from us, from me.

I knew what was going on, even if I didn't say anything. I was giving her time to come to grips with our new life. She had to realize that her place was here with us now. Me and Lilly.

But she was a stubborn woman and I know she would think she was betraying Rebecca's memory to build a life here. I wasn't asking her to marry me, but I could admit that I wanted to explore the possibilities. Every day she was here with me, my desire for her increased. I tried to hide it from her. Hell, I wanted to hide it from myself, but I couldn't any longer. I realized that now, but Norah wasn't. She was still fighting her place in our lives, and in our home.

As for me, I was a lost cause. I looked forward to seeing her face every morning. Her laughter made me smile. For a while, I'd forgotten what it felt like to just enjoy the sounds of life around me. But with Norah in the house, it had gotten easier again.

If I was being honest with myself, the few times she left out of town for work had been difficult. I'd called her each night on the pretense that Lilly wanted to talk to her, which wasn't a complete lie, but I wanted to hear her voice also. I wanted to know that she was safe in her hotel room with the door double locked every night. Until I had that last phone call with her at night, I couldn't rest. I worried about her so much I couldn't focus when she was away from home. When she returned, once I knew she was back at the house, that's when I could breathe again.

"You're a damn fool," I mumbled, taking the steps. "You lost your chance to have something with Norah all those years ago when you chose Rebecca. Stop wanting things to be different now."

But I couldn't stop thinking about her. Life was different now. I would always love Rebecca, but I also knew that I'd never stopped thinking about what could have been with Norah. The question is, am I strong enough to go after her?

Stopping in the hallway outside Norah's door, I raised my hand to knock. Then dropped it before turning away. What was I going to say? Were there any words that could make this better for her? Easier for her to accept? Just before I made it into my bedroom, I hesitated. Rubbing a hand along my chest, I reversed my steps and came back to Norah's door. I didn't know what to say, but that had never stopped me before. I'd think of something. Without giving myself a chance to backout, I knocked.

"Norah. We need to talk."

A few seconds passed before she opened the door. Her face was dry, but her eyes were red. At least she wasn't actively crying. I didn't think I could deal with that right now.

"Hey Cade," she said in a small voice. My heart clenched at the sound.

"Can I come in?"

She looked over her shoulder before opening the door wide for me to step through. "It's your house."

Defensive. Okay, at least I knew how she wanted to play this.

"No, it's our home. Yours. Mine. Lilly's."

"Rebecca's," she murmured.

I knew I needed to handle this the right way, or this would never go any further than where we are tonight. "Yes, this was Rebecca's home but she's no longer here. We both know this." Sitting on a chair across from the bed, I leaned over, my elbows on my thighs as I stared at her. Those long brown legs of hers and the painted red toes were in my line of sight. My eyes traveled from the bottom of her feet to the top of her head.

She was so fucking beautiful and there was no use denying how I felt any longer.

Opening my mouth, I began to speak. "When my letter arrived, I had no idea what to think. It was like she was speaking to me from the grave."

Norah's hands fidgeted with the hem of her shirt. "You said before that my letter was included with yours. I'm still confused about that and why you didn't give it to me right away?"

I shifted my gaze to her face. "Well, let's just say that Rebecca knew more than she let on. In her letter to me, she asked me to wait to give it to you. That I'd know the right moment."

"I still can't believe... I mean, the things she said." Norah looked into my eyes for a moment, then turned her head away. I knew that look.

Shame.

"Rebecca was never one to pull punches. She seemed like one of the quietest people you could know, but she never hesitated to speak her mind. She was tiny but she was like a firecracker when she felt passionate about something."

Norah laughed. "Without her, I probably wouldn't have done half the things I've experienced in my life. She would challenge me to do these crazy things. For our twenty-first birthday, we took a trip to Vegas. Did you know that?"

I nodded. "I did. She told me it was three of the best days of her life."

A smile came over Norah's face and I couldn't help but grin in return. "It was for me, too. I don't think we got more than four hours of sleep that entire weekend. She'd always tell me that sleep was for the weak and since we were strong, badass women, we didn't need no stinkin' sleep."

I stayed quiet. Norah was working through some things, and my role right now was to sit and listen.

"We went bungee jumping, did a pole dancing class. Ziplining on Fremont Street. Strip clubs… men and women. Nothing was off-limits that weekend. We were determined to create memories that would last a lifetime." She looked up at me with those brown eyes and I got lost. "And we did, Cade. I mean, I thought

I was going to die a few times, but it was so much damn fun. She had so much life in her and since she was my best friend, being around her gave me a chance to live."

She paused, breathing deep, the letter still trembling in her hands. I remembered the words from my own letter and tried to say something to take away the sadness.

"She wants you to still live. She's not here but you are. There's a whole life ahead of you, ahead of Lilly. You were her chosen one. And no matter how much we've had to adjust to a new way of living, we're still here. Alive."

"What are you saying?" She frowned over at me.

"I'm saying it's time for us, both you and me, to stop focusing on our pain. That's not what she would have wanted. She wants us to live. Whatever that means to you, it's time."

"Are you ready to start living again, Cade?"

I leaned back, not sure how to take that question. "I don't know what you mean?"

Her head tilted and she looked at me with a smile. "You're so busy working your business and taking care of Lilly, that you've become like a robot. You lost a part of yourself when she died."

Everything she was saying was true. For months, I walked around in a fog, angry at the world. Only when Norah came to live with us did I begin to come out of it. "Work is what kept me moving forward. Focusing on my business and creating the partnership with Overwatch Security was how I got out of bed every morning. That won't stop. Living comes in many different forms. My focus is on keeping my little girl happy."

Norah took a deep breath. "But what does that mean to you?"

This was something I was comfortable answering. "It means showing Lilly that she's loved. Giving her space to grow. Creating an environment where she can thrive. Stepping back when she needs you more than me. Giving you space to love her as a mother should."

Norah would be the only living Mother Lilly would know from this point on. Being with someone other than her was not an option for me. Even if Rebecca hadn't given her blessing, I had a strong feeling that I would have made my way to Norah on my own. Other than Rebecca, no other woman had called to me the way Norah did. When she was angry with me, I wanted to make her smile. Every time she was here at the house for those weekends, I'd wanted to ask her to stay. I just didn't think I had the right to take that step.

"I'm supposed to leave in three months." Looking around the room, she gave a low laugh. "I was scheduled to go back to

Baltimore. How can I be there for Lilly and live so far away again?"

Glancing down at my hands, I took a deep breath. "There's no reason for you to leave. The two of us, we're co-parenting at this point. It's not good to have you so far away from Lilly. She needs you here. I... need you here."

"Um... you want me to stay here with you?" She stood from the bed and began pacing.

I stood in return, because I wanted her to look me in the eyes as we continued talking. This was a moment of no return for us. "Norah, I want to ask you something."

She paused, looking up at me. I almost smiled but managed to hold it in. She was still so tiny compared to me. Standing six feet three inches and well over two-hundred-fifty pounds, I was a big man. Norah had to be no more than five feet six. I liked that she wasn't slim. No, she was curvy in all the right places. Hips. Ass. Breasts. Those plump juicy lips that I dreamed of at night.

"Cade? What did you need to ask me?"

Stepping closer, I looked down at her. "What would have happened if you'd been the one I talked to that night instead of Rebecca? Did you feel it as strongly as I did?" She went to step back, and I reached out to grab her arms. "No. Don't pull away. I just… I need to know." Talking to her now; being in front of her, I realized that I needed her answer.

Norah shook her head at me. "Cade. No. It's not fair of you to ask me that."

"Why not?"

"Because…" she paused, biting her plump bottom lip. "Because you already know the answer."

Closing my eyes for a moment, when I looked at her again, I could see her pupils dilated. Her breathing was heavier, her chest heaving with exertion. My gaze traveled down to her lips when her tongue peeked out to lick the dry flesh.

"I didn't know." Not sure if she understood what I was saying, I started over. "That night, when I lost sight of you, I thought it simply wasn't meant to be. Then I saw Rebecca."

Norah nodded her head as I spoke. "You made her happy."

"She made me happy, too. I don't regret marrying her." I wasn't going to disrespect my late wife by denying what I felt for her. That didn't mean I wasn't conflicted.

"The two of you made sense. That moment… it was just that. A moment. You and Rebecca had something real and I'm happy you were able to give her the life she wanted."

Shaking my head, I wanted her to stop talking. I didn't want to talk about Rebecca right now. This was about us, me and Norah. No one else. “I was faithful to my wife.”

She nodded. “I know that Cade.”

“Once I married Rebecca, I put aside thoughts of any other woman. I focused on my marriage. No matter how much I felt torn before I spoke my vows.”

Norah’s eyes widened but she kept on looking up at me. My hands were still wrapped around her upper arms. I could feel my dick hardening in my sweats. Her scent was irresistible—a hint of her perfume from earlier today combined with her unique musk. No matter how much I fought it, I couldn’t help leaning my head down towards her neck. Inhaling deeply, I groaned. “Fuck. You smell so good, Norah. I’m trying to resist it. I need to give you time.” I knew she wasn’t ready for everything I wanted.

It felt like I was pleading with her to pull me closer or even to push me away. I wanted her to do something that would give me a sign of how she was feeling.

"Forgive me." Exactly who I was apologizing to, I didn't know. Leaning down, I captured her lips with mine. The moment we kissed, I knew this was what I wanted, who I wanted. No matter how long it took, Norah would be mine.

Chapter 12

Norah

When his lips touched mine, I whimpered. Yup, a full-on whimper that could be heard for miles around. Okay, maybe that was just how it sounded to me. When he leaned down, all I could think was that I didn't want to fuck this up. Did my breath stink? Was there a pimple on my chin? Stupid shit.

I wanted this moment to be perfect. I didn't know when I'd get this chance again, so I needed to savor it. Embrace it. Bask in the glory that was Cade Donovan. My eyes were wide open because I didn't want to miss one second.

His kiss felt right. Time seemed to stop.

My feet lifted as I stood on my toes, trying to get closer to him. Pressing my body against his, I wanted to feel him.

His arms wrapped around my waist, pulling me tight against him. When his tongue came out to brush along my lips, coaxing them open, my knees buckled. Grabbing onto his arms with my hands, I relied on his strength to hold me up. The kiss was only a few seconds but then my mind started playing tricks on me.

Why was I kissing Cade?

What would Rebecca say? Actually, I know what she'd say. She'd already told me.

Bigger question is, why was he kissing me?

And although I wanted to pull back, I didn't.

Lifting my hands from his shoulders, I wrapped my arms around his neck. My fingers rubbed along his short hair. His lower body pressed into mine, his thick member pressing against my stomach. Hard. Hot.

That feeling was what jolted me back. I unwrapped my arms from around his neck and took a step away from him. My hands went to my mouth, covering my lips. "Cade? What are we doing? What are you doing? You're my best friend's husband."

He rubbed a hand along the back of his neck. His eyes bored into mine, freezing me in place. "Don't do that, Norah. We kissed. We both liked it. Stop acting like I'm cheating on Rebecca. I'm not."

I wanted to sink into the floor. This is what Rebecca was talking about in her letter to me. She knew that I'd been attracted to Cade, but did she think he was attracted to me also? No, that was impossible. I was the only fool in this scenario.

"It's the same thing. It hasn't even been two years since she's been gone."

Cade shook his head, his eyes going from me to the wall and back. “I know how long she’s been gone. I’ve lived with that knowledge every day.” He rubbed a hand down his face and took a deep breath. “Just forget this ever happened. Just chalk it up to a long day and a bad night. It was a mistake. It won’t happen again.” Standing in front of me, Cade stared down into my eyes for a few more seconds before he turned to leave. “See you tomorrow.”

“Yeah. See you tomorrow,” I couldn’t help but mumble in return.

After the bedroom door was closed, I leaned against it, breathing deeply. I’d kissed Cade. His arms were wrapped around my waist, holding me close to his muscular form. I’m not even gonna lie, it felt good. Even though I was fighting against the memory of his body pressed against me, I knew I’d be dreaming about it tonight and tomorrow and probably the next night after that.

"Rebecca," I spoke into the silence. "You know you've started some shit, right? If you were alive, I'd pinch you." After a few moments of silent laughter, I sobered up. "Then again, if you were here, Cade never would have kissed me in the first place."

Stepping away from the door, I climbed under the covers. That was enough excitement for the day. Now the question was, how would I face him tomorrow? Should I act normal? What if he wanted a repeat?

The Love Vixen told me I should give him the space he needed. He was still grieving, right? Was his grief the reason he'd kissed me? Maybe I was the closest thing he had to Rebecca?

Then again, we looked nothing alike, my dark skin to her pale skin. She'd had long blonde hair, while mine was dark, curly, and shoulder length. If I flat ironed my hair, it was much longer, but I hardly did that anymore.

Not unless there was a special occasion and I wanted to pull out a sleek look. I was an agitator, fighting against the system every chance I got, while Rebecca was quieter, more lowkey.

We were different in all the ways that counted when it came to looks and personality. There was no way Cade could be attracted to me after being with her for so long. But he kissed me…

"Ugh!" I flopped back on the bed. I was so confused.

No, I wasn't. I knew the best option was for me to stop acting like one kiss meant anything. It didn't. I tried to chalk it up to being just the heat of the moment. A slip up. Weakness. Need. Desire.

Yeah, those thoughts weren't really helping.

"Stop, Norah. Enough. You're not a teenager. You're a grown ass woman with responsibilities. You know how life works." Yet, here I was, talking to myself like a damn loon.

Giving up, I decided to just go to sleep and deal with it tomorrow. Cade had apologized… sort of. More importantly, he said it wouldn't happen again. That's what I wanted right?

I mean, what would our friends and family say if we started a relationship? Would they think this is something that had been going on when Rebecca was alive? Of course, nothing had happened then, and honestly, that little three-second kiss wasn't something that needed to be shared. If we kept it between the two of us, then there was nothing to worry about. I had no doubt Cade would do just that. With that final thought, I tried to relax. Everything would be fine, right?

The following morning, knocking woke me up. My body jackknifed in the bed

"Norah? Are you awake?"

It was Cade. Looking at the time display on my phone, I saw that it was a few minutes after nine in the morning.

Clearing my throat, I responded. "Uh... Yeah, I'm awake."

"I made breakfast."

What was up with this man and feeding me? I'd gained ten pounds since I've lived here.

"I'm going to pick up Lilly from her friend's house. I'll be back shortly."

Nodding, even though he couldn't see me, I flipped the covers back and climbed out of bed. "Okay, be safe."

"I will."

Then he paused. I know because I listened for the sound of him walking away.

After a few seconds, he spoke again. "Okay, I'll see you when we return."

“Okay.” So inadequate, but I heard his footsteps going down the stairs.

Was he waiting for me to say something else? Did he want to say more? Now we’d entered the awkward stage and that felt worse than the sexual tension filled, ‘I want you but can’t have you’ phase. Pulling out some underwear, a pair of shorts, and a t-shirt, I went into the bathroom to shower.

For the next twenty minutes, I wasn’t going to think about Rebecca’s letter or about Cade and his mesmerizing kisses and thick… muscles. Now if I could just decide how to handle him when he and Lilly returned.

I need to get my mind right, because if the opportunity came again for me to kiss Cade, I might be too weak to reject him. This entire situation was so confusing.

“You’re hopeless,” I muttered to myself, stepping into the shower.

Chapter 13

Cade

Sundays were supposed to be relaxed and easy. Not that I ever did any of that shit. Work never stopped for me, and today was no different. After picking up Lilly from her friend's house and returning home, I thought I'd spend an hour or so hanging out with her before heading into my home office.

If I were honest, I knew I wanted to explore this thing bubbling up between me and Norah. It was time for me to admit what I was feeling for the woman living in my home and helping me raise my daughter. She'd stopped me from losing my shit in those early days. I owed her so much. But it was more than that. I needed to confront what I was feeling every time I looked at her.

Even when she was snapping at me and rolling her eyes at something I'd said, I couldn't help but feel the pull. Today was no different. Everything in me wanted to be out there with her and Lilly, but I knew it would be a bad situation.

She came downstairs as me and Lilly returned. She was wearing a pair of shorts and a plain t-shirt. To anyone else, it would be an ordinary Sunday morning outfit. Perfect for staying inside and doing nothing. To me, it was pure temptation.

"Morning, Lilly! Did you have fun?" She knelt in front of my little girl. Her smile had caught me off guard, since I was expecting her usual standoffish reaction, especially considering what happened last night.

"Hi Auntie Norah. Yeah, we watched princess movies and then played dress-up and her mom made us chocolate chip pancakes."

Norah's smile stayed in place as she listened to my daughter. I had a sudden vision of her looking at me like that every day when I came home; a smile on her face, a secret in her eyes.

That kiss last night was something I'd dreamed about—the plumpness of her lips, the softness of her body. My hands gripped her so tightly, I'd be surprised if she didn't have bruises this morning. Just thinking about her made my cock thicken in my pants. Maybe I moaned a little or made some type of sound because Norah glanced up at me with a question in her eyes before turning back to Lilly.

"Sounds like the perfect night. How about we go put your stuff away?" Norah stood and then placed her hands on Lilly's shoulders. Glancing at me, she paused, licking her lips. It looked as if she were about to say something when Lilly interrupted. "Can we go to the park?"

Shifting her eyes from me, she glanced down at Lilly and nodded. "I think that would be perfect."

Feeling as though I had to interject, I tapped Norah on the arm to get her attention. "I have some work to do, but it can wait."

"No," she shook her head. "You do your thing. Let me take her. We'll be back in time to make lunch."

Lilly was already making her way up the stairs. Excited about going to the park, she must have gotten tired of waiting for us.

I stepped closer, bringing me within inches of Norah. "About last night..." Words failed me. What was I going to say? I'm sorry? No, because I wasn't sorry it happened. Finally getting a taste of her lips had felt good to me. Too damn good if I were honest. Was I going to say it wouldn't happen again? That would be a big ass hell no. I planned to kiss her again and again, and even more. I couldn't wait until I could have her naked underneath me. Now that was something I was looking forward to.

"What about last night?"

Norah didn't step away when she prompted me, but she did shift with nervousness. This close, I could practically feel the heat from her body. Looking down, I saw her nipples peeking through her thin t-shirt. My fingers itched to reach up and grab them, just to feel her flesh against mine.

Finally able to find the right words, I couldn't help staring at her lips. "I don't regret it."

Her eyes widened, but then she looked to the side for a moment before turning back to me. "I don't know if it's the smartest thing we've done, but I thought about it all morning, and…I don't regret it either."

I didn't even realize how much I'd been waiting for her response. At her words, my entire body relaxed. Relief flooded through me. Lifting my hand, I went to trace her jaw with my finger and paused. It was too soon. We weren't there yet, but I knew our day was coming. Returning my hand to my side, I could feel my lips tilting into a smile. "I plan for us to do it again." Might as well let her know exactly what I wanted.

As I said the words, I waited for the guilt to come. It didn't.

"Hold on there, buddy," she said with a smile on her lips. "Who said I wanted it to happen again?"

This time, I took a step forward. "Norah, you wouldn't deny me, would you?"

After a moment of pause, she took a small step back. "It's not about denying you. I think you know I enjoyed it just as much as you did. I just want to make sure we both know what we're doing."

"I know exactly what I'm doing. I'm just waiting for you to catch up."

"Auntie Norah!"

Norah jumped in surprise when Lilly called her name. Smirking, I took a step back. "This isn't over. We'll pick up this conversation later today." Turning to face the stairs, I saw my little girl standing at the top, changed into play clothes and sneakers.

"I'm ready for the park. Are you ready to go, Auntie Norah?"

"Um… yes, sweetheart. Just let me grab my shoes. Did you brush your teeth this morning?"

"Yes," Lilly said, spreading her lips in a large smile to show off her teeth. Not that we could see anything with her so far away, but she knew the drill.

Glancing over at Norah, I took in her outfit again, then I thought about all the men who would be at the park. "Are you wearing that? You need to change." There was no reason for her to be out like that, looking like a sumptuous treat, showing her body to others who had no right to look at her.

She looked at me with a raised eyebrow before looking down at her clothes. "Yeah. It's hot outside."

"Maybe you should change." It made no sense why I was choosing today to challenge her on what she wore. We'd lived in the same house for three months, and she'd spent every weekend here for more than a year before that. Before today, I'd never felt it was my place to exert my opinions about how she dressed. Then again, before last night, I didn't know what it felt like to kiss her, to have her body pressed up against mine, or know without a doubt that Norah was meant to be mine.

Everything in my world had shifted.

"I don't need to change, Cade."

I chuckled low under my breath. Even to my own ears, it sounded maniacal. "Oh, yes the fuck you do." Lilly had just arrived at the bottom of the stairs and was pulling on my hand.

"Daddy, are you coming to the park with us?"

Shaking my head, I leaned down to pick her up in my arms. "No, ladybug. Not today. But, while your auntie Norah changes clothes, why don't you tell me all about your night."

"I'm not changing, Cade."

I stopped, giving her a silent look, my eyebrow lifted as she challenged me. This is what I needed. What I missed. "Change on your own or I'll do it for you. But know that you're not going out like that. Not today. Not when I'm not with you. Since I need to stay here and do some work, then you need to change your clothes."

She scoffed, staring at me with a look of shock on her face. "You're serious."

"As a heart attack."

Norah stood there for a few more seconds but I ignored the look she gave to me. It was time for her to get to know the real Cade, not the façade I showed to the world every day. When I heard her stomp up the stairs, mumbling to herself, I couldn't help the smile that came over my face.

"Daddy, why's auntie Norah upset?"

Placing my daughter on the counter, I grabbed her a glass of water. "She's not upset, ladybug. She's just surprised that her life is changing faster than she expected." Maybe she thought it would be another three months before I moved things forward. After the past three years of my life, I was tired of waiting for something to happen. Life was too short. One day, you had your entire future ahead of you, and the next, you were lying in a bed waiting for cancer to finish ravaging your body.

It was time for me to live life on my own terms. I'd said my goodbyes to Rebecca, honored her memory and our life together. But I was still here. I was still alive, but I was also living a half-life. Wanting Norah, but not allowing myself to have her, had been killing me. Working long hours every day, 7 days a week, was not for me anymore.

A few minutes later, Norah came back downstairs. This time, wearing a pair of jeans. She'd even changed her top. She was still wearing a t-shirt, but it was of thicker material.

"Better," I quipped before lifting Lilly from the counter and placing her on the floor.

Norah rolled her eyes at me. "I'm not even sure why I changed. You don't get to tell me what I can wear Cade. This is ridiculous."

Shaking her head, she reached her hand out. "Come on, Lilly. Let's leave so your dad can get some work done."

"How long will you be?"

Picking up the keys to the SUV out front, she shrugged. "About an hour at the park, then I need to go to the market to get the items for lunch." Walking to the front door, she was about to exit when I stopped them.

"Norah?"

"Yes?"

"You changed because I asked you to. Because you know what this is. You may not realize it yet, but you'll give me what I want. Just like when you need something from me, I'll always give it to you. No matter what it is. I hope you're ready for that."

She stood frozen, mouth open, and eyes wide. It was best to get this out in the open. Life was about to change for her, for us, and I didn't want there to be any confusion about what was about to happen.

"Auntie Norah, come on," Lilly called out.

"Have fun, sweetheart. See you when you get back." I wasn't sure if I was saying that to Lilly or Norah. They were both my girls. I loved Lilly and I wanted Norah. During the past few years, I'd felt helpless as I watched life happen to me. Now it was my turn to make things happen for myself.

Once the door closed, I walked to my office, prepared to work for the next two hours so I could be ready to focus on my family when they returned. I turned on my computer and pulled up the latest proposal for Overwatch Security.

On Wednesday, I had a meeting with Stefano Indellicati, the founder and CEO, plus a few other owners. This deal had become more significant than I expected when I'd first began working with them. They'd referred me to a few different businesses and things were looking up for me and my company.

Today was the first day in a long time, when work was not my primary focus. I had two beautiful girls who would be returning home in a couple of hours. It's time for me to move forward, grab hold of the future, and build something new.

I just hope Norah was ready to build that future with me.

Chapter 14

Cade

This was a bad decision. Norah wasn't ready. Even though all these thoughts were running through my mind, that didn't stop me from stepping outside on the deck. At the sound of the door closing, Norah looked over at me as the glass of wine she was nursing in her hand was held halfway to her mouth.

I walked over and sat down beside her. "She's finally asleep."

"How many stories did it take tonight?"

Lifting my tumbler of whiskey, I smiled. "Two."

Humming in response, Norah lifted her glass and took a sip. "She was excited that you were able to spend so much time with us today. Usually, you're locked away in your office."

Nodding in response, I knew what she said was true. "There was always something to do."

She stared at me over the rim of her glass. "What changed today?"

"Realized that life was passing me by. I've been waiting for a sign that things were going to be okay. That all the effort I'd put into my company and my life was worth it. Maybe it's something that's been building up inside. Lilly won't be this age forever. She's going to grow up and these moments will fade." I took a breath, then swallowed the rest of my whiskey. "Life is too short and I'm not willing to let it pass me by anymore."

We sat in silence for a bit before she spoke up. "Are we talking about more than your time with Lilly?"

Turning my head to look at her, I let my eyes travel from the top of her head to the bottom of her feet before capturing her gaze with mine. "Yes."

She sighed as she looked out over the backyard. The quiet went on a bit too long, and I wanted—no, I needed to know what she was thinking. "Talk to me, Norah."

Some might say it was too soon for me to be interested in another woman. That I hadn't grieved long enough. But no one can understand what I'm going through unless they've been there. To spend so much time saying goodbye, preparing for the end, when it comes, there's a bit of relief mixed in with the grief. It wasn't that I was out looking for another woman to enter my life. I wasn't. But sitting here with Norah as we talked about our day playing with my daughter, closing out the evening with a drink in hand, sitting on the deck, felt good. It felt right.

When I was with her, the pain didn't exist. I was able to breathe more easily. My laughter came quicker. Work stopped being my mistress. It was comfortable, but also a bit exciting. I didn't know what life had in store for me, but I knew I wanted Norah by my side when I figured it out.

I'd been watching her this entire time and I saw the emotions float over her face. Sadness. Happiness. Uncertainty, especially when she bit her lip and her eyes fluttered as she looked down. If it was time she needed, I would give her that. But I hoped at the end, she ended up where I already was.

"How come we never talked about that night we all met?"

Well, that wasn't what I was expecting but if this is what she needed, I was all in. "It never seemed like the right time. I'd connected with Rebecca, we started dating, then got engaged, and then got married. It wasn't something I wanted to bring up to you."

Shifting in her seat, she pulled her feet up and tucked them beneath her. Fully facing me, Norah no longer had that look of uncertainty on her face. "You asked me what I thought would have happened if you'd talked to me that night. Honestly, I don't know if I want to answer that."

"Why?"

Norah shrugged. "Because that would mean I would have changed the past. You wouldn't have married Rebecca or had Lilly. It seems like a betrayal to what the two of you had."

Nodding at her words, I knew exactly what she was saying. That one moment in time. Fifteen minutes changed the course of my life. Could I have pursued Norah at the time? Probably? But after she'd seen me hugged up on her friend, I doubted that would have been something she'd respond to. No, I couldn't regret what I'd done.

"Norah, this isn't a betrayal. This is recognizing that there's something between us now. Today. It wasn't our time eight years ago. That doesn't mean we don't get a second chance." Deciding it was time to come clean with some of my own secrets, I rubbed a hand down my face before leaning over to rest my elbows on my knees.

"Her letter to me… she knew there was something between us."

Norah's gasp was loud in the night air. "But there wasn't…"

I nodded. "She knew that too. Rebecca wasn't accusing us of anything. She wanted me to know that it was okay to live. That she wanted me to find happiness… preferably with you."

As I waited for her to digest that bit of news, I sat in silence. Then I wondered if we'd ever be able to truly move beyond our past. Would every conversation involve discussing

Rebecca? When would we be able to just focus on us, our relationship? Was I fooling myself into thinking we could build something?

"Cade, my letter said something similar. She mentioned that she realized it later, that we'd seen each other that night."

I laughed, then lay my head back and looked up at the night stars. I'm not a man known for soft words, but I couldn't help but thank my late wife for what she was trying to do. Even though she was no longer here, she was still looking out for us, using everything within her power to bring me and Norah together.

Lifting my head, I looked over at the woman sitting next to me. The moonlight reflected down on her, giving her skin a light glow. Her brown eyes stared at me, a small smile on her lips. There was nothing I wanted to do more than to kiss her, claim her mouth again as I did the other night. Would she taste of the wine she was drinking? Would she return my kiss as strong as she did last night?

Damn, had it only been twenty-four hours since I'd kissed her? It didn't matter. I wanted more. Needed more.

"Norah, I want to kiss you again," I admitted. "Will you give me what I want?" My voice was low, guttural, and filled with need. Standing from the chair, I walked over in front of her. "If you don't want this, or want me, then tell me now. I'll back off. We'll forget what was in those letters and I'll never bring this up again. The two of us will focus on raising Lilly together, but separately." My hand reached out to her. "But if you want this as much as I do, or want me as much as I want you, then come to me. Stand up. Let me kiss you. Let me show you how much I need you."

She looked up at me for so long, I thought she was trying to think of a way to refuse my request. But then she placed her hand in mine, untucked her feet, and stood in front of me.

"Then kiss me," she demanded.

Without waiting a moment longer, I leaned down, capturing her lips with mine. My arms wrapped around her waist, pulling her closer to me. My lower body pressed into her, and I felt a jolt of electricity soar through me. Her taste, the softness of her lips, and the coconut scent of her body wash had overwhelmed me but at the same time, the mixture was perfectly balanced.

When she'd come home, she'd put on those shorts I'd demanded she change out of earlier today. Gripping her tightly, I lifted her. "Wrap your legs around me." The raw need in my voice came across loud and clear.

"Don't drop me," she whispered.

"Baby, I'm never gonna let you go again," I swore to her as I walked inside, made my way up the stairs and towards her bedroom. Once inside and the door was closed, I went over to her bed. "Norah, I want you tonight. I know we haven't resolved everything between us, but I need you." She bit her bottom lip, and I felt my dick throb in response. I bet she had no idea what she did to me, how she made me feel with just a look.

"I want you, too. We'll take things one step at a time. Let's just focus on right here, right now."

"Whatever you want." Hell, at this point, I would have agreed to just about anything she asked of me. I'd been tempted by her for so long. To finally have this moment, to have her underneath me, I was going to savor every second. She may think we would take this slow, but I had no intentions of letting her get away from me. Tonight would be the beginning of something amazing.

Gazing down at her, I kissed her again, my tongue delving inside her mouth. I needed her taste. I needed to be connected to her. We were wearing too many clothes. I ached to feel her bare flesh against mine. My hand roamed up and down her body, touching her everywhere I could. When she lifted her legs higher, it tilted her lower body, pressing her hot center against me. I broke away from the kiss, pushing my head into the space between her neck and shoulder. “Fuck. You feel so good. Not enough. I need more.”

“Cade,” she whispered my name.

I closed my eyes at the sound and basked in the feeling of being with Norah. Trailing my lips down her chest, I lifted her shirt, baring her stomach to my gaze. I licked her skin, memorizing her taste on my tongue. My mouth began to water in anticipation. Lifting from her, I pulled my shirt off before shifting my attention to her clothes. Within minutes, she lay in front of me wearing only a pair of skimpy black underwear. I placed my nose at the juncture of her thighs and inhaled.

"Cade?"

"Don't interrupt me," I growled. My tongue flicked out and tasted her through the fabric. She was already so wet for me. Her panties were already soaked with her essence. Her flavor exploded on my tongue and my dick throbbed in my pants, begging me to come out and play.

"Oh, fuck," she moaned.

"Exactly." With swift movements, I grabbed her underwear and removed them from her body. Flinging the material over my shoulder, I stared down at her bare mound. It was my new favorite view; puffy brown lips with a warm pink center. Norah moved to raise her upper body and I placed one of my hands in the middle of her chest. "No. Lay back. You have no idea how many times I've dreamed of having you here like this. Let me enjoy the sight of you."

Norah whimpered, her lower body squirming as my hot gaze seared into her. "Please."

That one word did it for me. Placing my head between her thighs, I swiped at the moisture clinging to her skin and moaned. Damn, she tasted good. Going in deeper, I used my mouth to swipe and lick her nether lips. Plump and juicy. Her cream began to flow, and her moans became louder. Shifting my hand from her chest, I went to cover her mouth when she grabbed it. Pulling my fingers into her mouth, she sucked at my digits as if they were another part of my anatomy.

Wrapping my other hand around her leg, I pulled her closer to me as my mouth devoured her. Norah had no idea that after tonight, she would be mine. No one would interfere with us again. Now that I finally had her, there was nothing that would stop me from making her my woman.

I may have been blinded to what was right in front of me, but no more.

When she pulled my hand away from her mouth, her body began convulsing. "Oh. Shit. Yes, Cade. I'm coming. Oh, gawd."

Every word from her mouth was like music to my ears.

Pulling her hardened clit in between my lips, I sucked on the sensitive flesh as my tongue joined the party, flicking against the hardened nubbin. It pulsed. She slapped her hands across her mouth. Body tensing, her hips arched. My eyes were trained on her, taking in every second of this moment.

Norah's toes curled. I grabbed her ass, pulling her lower body closer. I didn't want to miss a moment as she broke apart in my arms.

"Yes. Yes. Yes," she whined.

Then her body released ambrosia and I swallowed every fucking drop. Fuck, yes. She was mine. After so many years, she was finally going to be mine. Even though she may try to fight it, we both knew tonight would change everything.

Norah belonged to me.

Releasing her, I lifted from the bed to remove my pants. I needed to be inside her.

Chapter 15

Norah

The first touch of his tongue against my lower lips set me off. I felt like stars were exploding behind my eyes. I wasn't a virgin, and I'd done plenty of things in bed with my previous partners. But it was something about the feel of his wet appendage pressing against my clit, licking, sucking, and kissing, that made me float away.

I wanted to get closer to him. I *needed* to get closer to him. The sounds he made caused goosebumps to rise along my skin, which made me even hotter for him. My hands clenched at his hair, but it was too short for me to grab hold. My thighs shook and I lifted my hips. Oh, if he could just hit that one spot... Yeah, that was it. It was like he was reading my mind.

"Oh. Yes," I moaned. I grabbed at the bed and my voice became louder the more he focused on bringing me pleasure. I needed him to never, ever stop. When I got louder, he tried to cover my mouth with his hand. It was time for a bit of payback. I used my oral skills to give him a preview of what it would feel like with my mouth, pleasuring him the way he did me. I must have been doing a good job because he moaned against my pussy.

"Fuck, Cade. Yes!" How could one man know how to hit every single button? I could do this all night. Well, his mouth might get tired after a few hours, but I could live just like this and be a happy woman.

My lower body squirmed as I pressed my mound closer. Glancing down my body, I saw his hot gaze watching me and it set off something inside of me. I wanted him. I wanted this. It didn't matter what others would say, my place was with Cade. In his home. In his bed. Picturing what a future would look like with him by my side caused me to whimper. "Please."

I could swear the man grinned. He wrapped his arms around my thighs, pulling me closer. Swipe. Lick. Nibble. Plunge. Ecstasy coursed through my body, my stomach tightened, my toes curled, and I could feel my channel begin to clench as my orgasm ripped through me. One leg arched in the air as my body seized.

It felt like I was floating in midair. My breath was caught in my lungs. My eyes were open, but I was blinded by the feeling rushing through me. Tears fell from my eyes. I was overwhelmed. Then he wouldn't stop, and I experienced minor aftershocks. My hands went to push him away when he separated from my body.

Shifting back, he quickly removed his pants and underwear before standing before me in all his glory. If I thought he was sex on a stick before now, this confirmed it for me. I wanted to lick every inch of his body.

As he looked down at me, one eyebrow arched and a smirk on his lips, I knew I was in trouble. When my eyes fell to his manhood hanging between his legs, I gasped. Well, fuck me… no, literally. I wanted him to fuck me.

It was beautiful.

Thick.

Veiny.

Long.

And just at the tip, there was a bead of liquid.

I wanted him inside me, but I could also admit I was a bit fearful. Okay, I wasn't a virgin, but I'd only had a few sex partners. None of them… not one… was as thick or long as the man in front of me. As my legs began to close, I felt Cade place a hand on my knee.

"What're you doing, Norah. Don't get shy on me now." Then he had the nerve to laugh at me.

Shifting my body back, I pointed at him. "You and that monster need to step back.

"Baby, we're not going anywhere." He climbed on the bed and the way he came toward me, reminded me of a lion stalking his prey. "Come here and give me that pretty kitty," he purred. Maybe not a purr, but I felt that his words were hypnotizing me.

And then I melted. Yes, I mean that. Like my body turned into a big pile of mush and felt trapped in his gaze. His hand rubbed along my leg before lifting it and spreading it wide. As he brushed along my naked form, he took the time to place a soft kiss at the top of my pulsating mound. The memory of the orgasm he'd given me was so fresh in my mind, my body jerked up toward him. Maybe if I asked nicely, he'd do it again.

When he continued up, I groaned in need and defeat.

He laughed as he placed a soft kiss on my stomach. “One day,” I heard him whisper.

“What?”

Shaking his head, he whispered, “We can talk about it later.” He continued his journey up my body, licking at my breasts before placing his mouth on one nipple, sucking and biting, before turning his attention to the other. “Tasty.”

“Cade? Are you…?” I had to pause because he took his tongue and swiped from the bottom of one breast all the way to the top. “Um…”

Fitting his body against mine, I could feel the tip of his thick member as it brushed up against my heated core. If my pussy could talk, she’d be begging and pleading for him to come on inside.

He leaned down to kiss me, and I could taste my essence on his lips. It was intoxicating. I watched as he licked his lips. Lifting one hand to trail it down his face, I wrapped my hand around his chin, gathering his dark beard, and pulling down.

"Now, no more talking. Just enjoy the ride," he said before sliding inside me. My mouth fell open as the first inch spread me open. I closed my eyes and grabbed onto him with my hands. "Yeah, that's it. Hold on to me, Norah." Cade gathered my legs in the crook of his arms and pressed forward, opening me wider for his breach.

"Oh," I gasped.

"Yeah, baby. It's gonna be a tight fit, but you got this."

He twisted his hips while pressing in further. It felt like I was being split open and put back together at the same time. Why did he feel so good? As he thrust slowly inside me, tears of joy gathered in my eyes. Even as he whispered encouraging words to me and told me to just let it happen, I wanted to wrap my arms and legs around him and never let go.

If this is what it felt like to be with him, I never wanted it to stop.

He pulled back slightly and pushed in even deeper. “Oh, yeah. You feel so good, Norah. I knew you were meant for me. You’re so beautiful, Norah. I’m not letting you go. No one will get in between us again.”

All I could do was nod because I agreed with everything he said. Once he reached as far as he could, he paused.

“I’m not leaving this bed tonight,” he said before kissing me softly.

“No one asked you to.” I twisted my hips to get a better position, but he stopped me.

“Don’t move. I want to make love to you this first time. Next time it’ll be a hard fucking. There are so many things I want to do with you, but this first time is all about showing you how much I want to worship you. I want to love you. I want you to know that from this day forward, I belong to you, and you belong to me.

"Cade—" before I could finish saying his name, he'd pulled out and thrust back inside me. "Oh!"

No other words needed to be said because he took me to heaven in 1.2 seconds. Every stroke touched my soul. Every time he went deep inside me, I wanted to call him a sex god. He was like a machine. There was no slowing down. He twisted, grabbed, and thrust like a man on a mission.

My eyes closed and I was blinded with ecstasy. All I could do was hang on, my nails ripping into his back as he pounded inside me. Damn, this man fucks so good. As I had that thought, I felt my second orgasm rushing through me. I moaned low and I heard Cade speak.

"There it is," he said lifting his head to stare down at me. "Make that sound again." He did something with his hips, and I felt as if my body was filled with light. My head fell back and a deep sound, one I'd never heard before, released from my throat. "Yeah, baby. You're all mine," he growled.

I careened toward the finish line. Did I care that Cade wasn't finishing with me? Not really. Right now, I was focused on the pleasure I was feeling. He'd catch up. My hot channel clenched around him as he stilled above me. Just as I was about to catch my breath, he pulled out, and flipped me over.

"All fours, Norah." He rubbed a hand down my bare ass. When he slapped my flesh, I yelped. Before I could register the full extent of the pain, he leaned down and kissed me. "Next time you tell me to kiss your ass, don't be surprised when I do it."

Giggling, I looked over my shoulder, ready to say something sarcastic. One look at his face and my mouth slammed shut. Cade did not look like he was in a joking mood. Intensity filled his eyes as he stared down at my body underneath his.

"Cade?"

When his eyes lifted to look at my face, the look faded somewhat. "Yeah, baby?"

"You okay?" Butterflies took flight in my stomach.

Nodding, he placed one hand in the middle of my back and pressed down, while his other hand grabbed his dick. "I'm better than okay. I'm fucking perfect." Sliding all that thickness inside me again, he hissed out my name. "Norah… fuck, baby."

My back arched as I moaned in response. Resting my head on the bed, placing my arms to the side, I awaited his next move. This position must have given him more depth because it felt like he was further inside than before. I could feel him in my stomach and that caused my body to react, jerking and moving as another orgasm flowed through me. "Cade. Please move."

I was dickmatized. Hypnotized by the dick and I wasn't going to apologize for it.

Shifting the hand on my back, he grabbed a fistful of my curly hair and pulled, just as he thrust harder inside me. I squealed. He laughed. Fucking sexy ass motherfucking sadist.

Something was let loose at that moment because Cade didn't let up. His pace was steady, deep, focused. I tried squirming away, but he smacked me on the ass, not allowing me an inch.

"Don't you run from me. You need to take all this dick. This is yours now, baby. Say it," he said on a hard thrust. "Tell me that you know I belong to you. Tell me, Norah."

Even as he fucked me into oblivion, I fought against saying the words. As soon as I said what he wanted, there would be no returning. Going back to the way things were wouldn't be an option. But, damn, he felt good. Cade was asking me… no, he was telling me; I was his and he was mine. Was I ready to accept it?

He reached a hand around and rubbed my clit as he thrust harder and harder. "Tell me what the fuck I need to hear, Norah, or I'll stop right now. Give me what I want, and I'll give you what you need." Cade backed up his words and began to slow down.

"No! Cade, please." Yes, I was blubbering like a damn fool. Now that I'd had this, could I give him up? No, that wasn't possible anymore, so I gave him the words. "You belong to me, Cade. I belong with you."

"Yes, you sure as hell do," he growled before picking up the pace, hitting all the right places inside my body. "You're mine now."

There was no use in responding. The tears flowing from my eyes, the orgasm crashing through my body, and my continuous moans gave him all the answers he needed. When I felt him grow even more, stretching my body wider, I knew he was about to finish.

"Yes, please," I moaned. Maybe we'd make a little brother or sister for Lilly. As I finished the thought, he exploded inside me, his warmth filling me.

Chapter 16

Cade

More than two weeks later and I couldn't get enough of Norah, of being with her, kissing her at night, sinking inside her body in her bed. We hadn't yet slept in my room. I had my thoughts on why she wasn't ready for that and had no choice but to accept it. I wasn't going to push her if she didn't feel comfortable. Even though she and I both wanted this, I knew she was still working through things when it came to our relationship.

But every night, when she was in my arms, looking up at me with those gorgeous brown eyes, and pulling me close as I repeatedly claimed her body, I knew what we had was real. We were still careful about showing affection around Lilly. Before we took that next step, I wanted to make sure Norah was comfortable with where things were headed for us.

Next Saturday would be our first test. The owners of Overwatch Security invited me to a charity event they were hosting for survivors of domestic violence. It was a well-publicized story that the founder's wife was a survivor, and one of the company's other executives had a sister who was killed by her husband. So when the invitation came through to me earlier today, there was no doubt in my mind about if I would go.

I would even put on the damn tuxedo that was required since it was a black-tie event. A bonus was that the invite allowed me to bring a plus-one. Norah would be by my side, in public, for the first time since we officially became a couple. She'd been hesitant to share our new relationship dynamics with others because she was still concerned about the optics.

Me, I didn't give a shit about what other people thought. I wasn't giving her up for anyone, so they could go fuck themselves if they had a problem with the two of us being together. I had been lucky enough to find love twice in my life. Nothing was going to stop me from having the woman I wanted in my arms.

Tonight had been a late night at the office and I wasn't happy about getting home late. A look at my watch showed that it was past eight, which meant Lilly was already in bed. I opened the door to my house, and I listened for a moment but all I heard was silence. Then I made my way into the living room, I placed my case on the table and slid off my suit jacket. Since I had client meetings all day, I had to dress in this monkey suit, which I really didn't enjoy. Jeans and a button up shirt were my usual attire when I made it to the office. Pulling my sleeves back, I called out. "Norah? You down here?"

When I made it into the kitchen, I saw a note on the counter waiting for me.

Cade,

Dinner is in the microwave.

Dessert is upstairs.

Norah

Well, damn. Was there really any other choice for me. Dessert had always been my favorite meal of the day.

Placing the note back on the counter, I took out two bottles of water from the refrigerator. Once I made sure the house was locked up, I jogged upstairs to Norah's bedroom. I didn't bother knocking because I knew she heard me come inside the house and make my way upstairs.

I popped into Lilly's room to make sure she was covered with a blanket. I gave her a small kiss on her forehead and exited her room.

Once I made my way into Norah's room, my eyes were immediately drawn to the bed and the sight in front of me. Closing the bedroom door, I placed the water bottles on the dresser and walked over to stand next to the bed.

She looked up at me, a smirk on her lips, and lust in her eyes. "Hey, Cade."

Norah was propped on the bed, her knees bent, and legs spread wide. I had a clear view of her bare mound. She wore one of my ties… my favorite one. It was the only piece of material covering her body. My dick jumped, filling out and growing in anticipation.

"Norah."

"Did you eat dinner?"

Removing my tie, I began to undress. I don't know how long it took, but it felt like only a few seconds before I stood in front of her naked. “I’m about to eat dinner and dessert right now.” Grabbing one leg, I opened it wider before taking my hand and trailing a finger up her slit. Wetness coated my finger. Lifting the digit to my mouth, I sucked her essence off before dipping my hand between her legs again. “Is this for me?”

A shiver went through her body as she closed her eyes. “Yes.”

“Good girl,” I praised her. How I could have lived without her in my life, and in my bed, was still a mystery to me. “I like it when you’re up here waiting for me.”

Norah lifted one hand and cradled my jaw. Turning my head, I kissed her palm as I continued positioning myself on the bed. Tilting her head, I kissed her softly, sucking her tongue into my mouth. She tasted of sweet bubblegum. She broke the kiss as she continued looking into my eyes.

“I like it when you come home to me at night. I figured you deserved a little surprise for taking such good care of us every day.”

“Damn, baby. That’s what I’m talking about.” Laying between her legs, I prepared to drive my woman crazy.

Two hours later, we were both tired, sweaty, and thirsty.

“I’m glad you liked my surprise,” she said, swirling her fingers in the hair on my chest. “Your chest hair is so soft.”

Thoughts of other conversations about my chest hair filtered into my brain. Not everyone liked a man like me. I was rough around the edges, cursed too much, didn’t mince my words, and didn’t really give a shit about anyone except my family. I would never be that polished business owner that graced the cover of magazines. With me, what you see is what you get.

"I'm glad you like it." I wouldn't apologize for who the hell I was. Norah wanted me just the way I was, and she was the only one who mattered.

Norah shifted, wrapped up in the sheet, she looked over at me. "Are you hungry?"

Smirking, I wrapped my arms around her waist and pulled her back against me. "Baby, I thought you were tired. If you're ready for round four, all you have to do is ask."

She laughed, slapping me lightly on the arm. "What? No! I meant are you hungry for food, from the kitchen? You never did eat the meal I had waiting for you."

"I didn't need that meal. There was a whole snack upstairs waiting for me." I loved teasing her, especially about sex. Norah claimed I was insatiable, but I also knew she loved every single minute of my appetite for her. I would never tire of being inside her, so she'd better get used to it.

"Cade... you know what? You can starve." She plopped back on the bed.

Leaning over to suck at the skin of her neck, I inhaled her unique scent, plus mine mixed in. It was something I would never get tired of. "Actually, I am hungry. Want anything?"

"Ice cream," she blurted out. "I got some pralines and cream at the store earlier. I was going to save it for tomorrow, but since you're asking."

Standing from the bed, I put on a pair of sweats that I left in here for easy access. "Coming right up." Exiting the room, I made it back to the kitchen. While my food was warming up, I put a few scoops of ice cream in a bowl for the Queen Bee upstairs.

As I stood there waiting, I realized that I was happy again. Not that giddy-childhood crush type of happiness, which isn't something that would ever apply to me. But I was happy with Norah, our life, and content to be at home.

After Rebecca died, I'd been restless. All I wanted to do was work, hang out with my daughter, and work more. Now, my focus was on getting home to Norah and Lilly as fast as I could. Staying in the office late no longer held any appeal for me. It was… different… than it had been before. Back when things were normal, before Rebecca got sick, I felt that my work, my business, is what made me worthy of her love. That if I provided a good home for my family, then that made me worthy.

After it all went to shit, I realized that no amount of money could make things better. It didn't matter how much cash I threw at the situation, my wife was going to die, and there was nothing I could do about it.

As I think about it now, I knew that I never would have made it to this point without Norah being there for me, for Rebecca. Almost a year later, I knew that I'd finally made it to the other side. I was ready for whatever was to come.

I'm stronger.

I'm wiser.

I'm better.

When I look back at all I've gone through, I can now see that Norah was the one I held on to, the one who kept me going.

Could I have lost it all, lost a future with her, if I hadn't opened my eyes? If I hadn't received that letter? I probably would have lost my mind, wallowing in my grief and pain. I guess it's a good thing I surrounded myself with strong, beautiful women.

When the microwave dinged, I pulled out the plate, grabbed the ice cream, napkins, and utensils, and made my way back upstairs.

As we were lying in bed, I glanced over at Norah. "Thank you."

Scooping another bite of ice cream into her mouth, she spoke around the icy goodness. “You’re welcome… but for what?”

“For being here for me and for Lilly. For loving my daughter. For returning here when I asked you. Norah, I never would have made it this far without you.”

I saw her eyes shimmer as she swallowed.

“No, baby. I didn’t mean to make you cry.”

“I’m not crying. Well, not because I’m sad. These are happy tears.”

Laughing, I used one hand to wipe the wetness that began to trail down her face. “Well, whatever the reason, stop it. When I see tears in your eyes, I want to fuck some shit up.”

My heart felt like it was being squeezed between a vice grip. I didn’t care what the reason was for her tears, I didn’t like it.

"Cade, you can't tell me to not cry if I'm happy."

I moved my empty plate to the side. I'd take the dishes downstairs later. "Yes, I can. Haven't you heard about me? Hell, I'm the famous Cade Donovan."

"Yeah, more like infamous," Norah giggled before setting her bowl down, grabbing me around the waist, and placing her head on my shoulder.

I grabbed one of her legs and I pulled it tight. "This Saturday, we have a dinner to attend. It's a charity event being sponsored by Overwatch."

Her hands were rubbing along my chest hair again, but she paused. "Isn't that the company you've been working with these past few months? The one that brought you those new clients?"

Proud that she remembered, I nodded. "Yes, those are the ones. It's to benefit and support survivors of domestic violence."

"What do I have to wear?"

"It's black tie. Do you already have something to wear, or do we need to buy you a dress?"

She shook her head. "I think I do. But if I don't, I'm not going to ask you to buy me anything. I already live here rent free. Do you realize how much money I'm saving by being here? Getting out of my apartment lease was one of the best decisions I could have made."

She thought she was going to slide that smart ass comment in without me noticing. "Norah, if you need a dress, I'm going to buy it for you. Doesn't matter if you have six-figures in your bank account. Let me do this for you."

I heard her make some noncommittal sound. This was another way Norah was different, she never wanted to use my money.

I had plenty of it and was continuing to make more. I wanted her to lean on me when she needed something; to be in a fully committed relationship. Then understanding dawned. She was still fighting it—fighting us being together as a couple. This needed to change, because this half-in / half-out bullshit wasn't working for me anymore.

Chapter 17

Norah

Was I nervous about tonight? Yes.

It was the first time we were going to be out together, publicly, as a couple. Because this was a charity event with some work colleagues, I wasn't overly concerned, but still.

Putting the final touches on my make-up, I looked in the mirror and smiled at the woman staring back. My dress was an off-the-shoulder, royal purple, floor length gown. A split on the side showed off my toned brown leg up to the middle of my thigh. The waist was cinched tight with a side clasp, giving me an old-time elegance.

I was about to walk out of my room when I heard a knock on the door just before Cade walked in. As my eyes trailed up his body, I couldn't help the desire that flared to life. He wore a classic tuxedo with a black bowtie. On any other man, it wouldn't catch my attention. On Cade, it was a different situation all together. He looked… breathtaking. He'd probably laugh if I said that out loud, but it was the truth.

Walking over to me, he stopped just inches away. "So beautiful."

When he looked at me with those green eyes and that half-smirk on his lips, I wanted to melt in his arms. Every day, I fell even deeper in love with him. Sometimes, when we woke up in bed together, before Lilly started her day, I couldn't believe everything that had happened. Cade, in bed with me, his arms wrapped around my naked waist, his flaccid cock coming to life as he pressed up against my bare ass.

Lifting my face to his, I met him halfway as he gave me a light kiss. "Thank you. You don't look so bad. I guess you'll do," I teased.

"Woman, I look damn good in this monkey suit. I can't wait until we can leave. Make sure you stay by my side tonight."

I pulled away from him to pick up my small evening purse. "Why?" Moving around the room, I took one final look in the mirror before exiting the space. Cade was right behind me.

"Because with how that dress is hugging your curves, I don't want to have to punch one of these rich fucks who thinks they can press up on you."

I laughed as I glanced over my shoulder, then we made our way downstairs. "Stop, Cade. No one's going to be thinking about me. You, on the other hand, may have to fight women off. You look very... tasty tonight."

Facing front, I couldn't help the smile that came over my face when I heard him growl.

"Keep on talking shit and we'll never make it to this event."

That would be just fine with me, but I held back from saying it. This event was important to Cade's business. The connections he made tonight could help him shift his company to the next level. There was no way we were going to miss it.

Even if I still wasn't sure how long we would last, or what was happening in our relationship, I knew that I wanted to do this for him. I loved Cade and Lilly. They were my family. If schmoozing with people who had pockets deeper than the Grand Canyon would help Cade, then that's what we were going to do.

Just as my feet hit the main floor, I heard Lilly call out. "Auntie Norah, you look like a princess."

Walking over to the little girl, I grabbed her in my arms for a hug. "Thank you, ladybug. Now, you be good for Stacy."

Lilly nodded at the smiling teenager standing off to the side. Over the past few months, Stacy watched Lilly two or three times a month if Cade had a late night and I was traveling. Her family lived across the street, and she was entering her senior year of high school. She was a lovely young lady and never hesitated to watch Lilly when we needed her. It probably helped that Cade paid her more than the going rate. All I know is that it worked for us and that's what mattered.

"Stacy, we won't be too late," I addressed the young lady. "No later than eleven."

"Yes, ma'am. We already have a movie picked out for the night."

Nodding, I cupped Lilly's face in my hands. "Bedtime no later than nine. You get one story… okay, maybe two, but that's it. Be a good girl while we're out." I stood to my full height before glancing over at Cade, who came over to us.

"Yes, auntie Norah. But, if the movie goes past nine, can I stay up then?"

Little imp. "Cade?"

Shaking his head, he ran his hand down his daughter's hair. "Pick a movie that won't go past your bedtime. Stacy, you're in charge, not the little princess here."

Lilly poked her lip out before wrapping her arms around Cade's waist. "Okay, Daddy."

"I love you, ladybug. We'll be back later.

"Night Mr. Donovan, Ms. James."

Waving, we made our way out of the house and to the car waiting for us at the curb. Since we'd both probably be drinking, Cade chose not to drive tonight. "You know she's gonna stay up past her bedtime, right?"

A smile lifted his lips as he placed his hand at the small of my back. "Definitely. To be so young, that girl has the gift of negotiation. I don't know where she gets it from."

I tried to ignore the heat permeating through my dress where his hand caressed me. It would do no good to lose myself in his touch tonight. It was too early, and we had a whole night ahead of us.

"Oh, she gets it from her momma. Rebecca could convince me to do just about anything. Half the trouble I got into in my teens and young adult years was because of her. So, be ready for what's coming your way."

Once we arrived at the door, cade took my hand as I climbed inside. "Don't worry. We'll handle it together. She'll have both of us and as long as we stick together, it'll be fine."

It's a good thing I was looking away from him because I'm sure my face reflected the shock I felt inside. I knew I was behaving like one of those foolish women who couldn't believe her good fortune. Him speaking so freely about us raising Lilly together surprised me. Then again, maybe he was only referring to me being her godmother, not he and I as a couple.

Maybe.

Once he was inside and the door closed, he turned to look at me. His eyes looked me up and down, his gaze lingering on my breasts, then my lips. “Have I told you how beautiful you look tonight?” He said while reaching over to grab my hand.

Dipping my head, I avoided his gaze. If I looked at him too long, I knew he’d recognize the need in my eyes. I couldn’t get enough. During the day, I counted down the hours until he returned from the office. Whenever I traveled, I dreaded being away from him overnight. It was like he was underneath my skin, changing me, molding me into someone else. A woman made just for him.

"Yes, you mentioned it a time or two," I finally managed to whisper.

"Not enough." Cade brought one hand to my face, using his forefinger to lift my chin. He slowly moved closer to me, pressing his lips to mine for a soft but quick kiss. "You are so beautiful. Every man in that room will wish he were me tonight. You're mine, Norah. Just in case you ever doubt how I feel about you, I want to make it clear. We belong together. Being with you feels so right, so good." He paused, looking into my eyes. "Do you believe me?"

Okay, so maybe I was exactly like all those women in the romance books. The man I'd wanted for so long, who made love to me every night, who told me with words and actions that I was the one he wanted... I still questioned if he meant what he said.

"Norah? Say you know that we belong together."

Staring off to the side, I took a deep breath. "Do you want honesty, or do you want me to tell you what you want to hear?"

I watched his shoulders fall as the look on his face hardened. "I want the truth," he snapped.

Pulling back, I finally looked into his eyes. What I saw there stopped the words from spilling. He looked… hurt. "I believe you. I believe that you want this to be true. I believe that you desire me, that you enjoy having me in your bed… or being in my bed," I tried to joke. He didn't smile.

Leaning back against the seat, Cade blew out a harsh breath. "Why can't you believe that I want you?"

Shaking my head, I tried to find the right words. This was getting all messed up and I had a feeling I was ruining our night. I didn't want that. "I know you want me, Cade. You prove that every night and morning." I smiled. He glanced over at me and smiled in return.

"Yeah, I do. There's nothing like waking up and feeling that ass pressed against me. All I want to do is slide inside you, make you moan my name again and again. It's the sweetest fucking sound in the morning."

If I were lighter, my face would be flaming red right now. Good thing we were in a dark car. If he could see the need reflected in my eyes right now, my dress would be flipped over my head and my legs wide open for him. "As you've so eloquently said, I know how much you want me. But I still question what happens to us two months or even two years from now. Will you still want me the way you do today?"

Grabbing my hand, he pulled me close. "Sweetheart, I don't know where this is coming from. Then again, maybe I do."

I think we both knew where this was coming from, but neither of us wanted to bring it up, but it didn't mean it wasn't something I worried about, something I didn't think about.

Was I still just a replacement for Rebecca?

Rubbing his thumb along the back of my hand, he sat in silence for a few minutes. "Norah, look at me," he said when my gaze fell to my shoes. They were nice shoes after all, silver, shiny, with a peep-toe design. At his words, I looked up as he requested.

"Baby, I'm here with you because I want to be. No matter what may have happened before, being here with you today, is where I belong. I know that big, beautiful brain of yours is still trying to come to grips with what's between us. I just wish you would see the truth in front of you."

Nodding, I tried to just hear his words and listen to what he was saying to me. I wanted to just be with him without all the worry filling my head. It was difficult. "I'm trying," I finally admitted.

"That's all I can ask. Just be in the moment with me."

"Okay." Just then, we pulled up to the Kennedy Center in Washington, DC where the event was being held. "This is a good night for you, Cade. I'm right here by your side."

"I know you are. Thank you, Norah."

We stared at each other for a moment, our nonverbal communication said more than words could. The driver opened the door for Cade to exit. He waited by the door, grabbing my hand to help. I held onto his proffered elbow as we walked up the stairs and into the building. There were lights, a red carpet and music welcoming us into the grand space. It felt like I was stepping into a whole new world. Maybe I was.

As we entered the space, I looked around in awe, amazed at how everything had been transformed. Oh yeah, there was some big money in the room tonight. Not only would the domestic violence cause benefit, but I had a feeling tonight would change everything for Cade.

He whispered in my ear. "Would you like something to drink?"

"Yes, please." Just then, a waiter passed by, holding a tray full of champagne glasses. Grabbing one for each of us, he handed me mine.

With the clinking of our glasses, he toasted me. "To new beginnings, our future, and building something together."

My mouth fell open at his words. Oh, so he wasn't playing around.

"Close your mouth, Norah. Take a drink."

Lifting the glass, I took a drink, but I didn't taste the expensive liquid. His words were still floating around in my head. "To our future," I smiled up at him and went to lean in for a kiss when a voice interrupted us.

"Cade? Is that you? It's been such a long time." The brunette looked at him, then at me, then at Cade's arm around my waist. "I wasn't expecting to see you tonight, but I'm glad you're here. You don't come out enough now that your wife has passed." She looked at me again, her eyes seemed to widen in recognition. "Hi. I'm Sylvia Martin, an old friend of Cade's. You are?"

Glancing at Cade, I saw him looking down at me with a hard glint in his eyes. I turned back to the woman and reached out my hand. "I'm Norah James."

"Oh… I know that name. Aren't you the best friend of his late wife? Well," she glanced down at Cade and I standing so close together, "isn't this interesting."

And that's when the night went to hell in a handbasket.

Chapter 18

Norah

I didn't wait for Cade to let me out of the car. Jumping out from the other side, I stomped to the front door of the house. Now, imagine doing this while wearing five-inch heels. It was an accomplishment on its own, but throw in four glasses of champagne, hardly any food in my stomach, and an urge to slap someone. Yeah, I was on a tear. Behind me, I heard Cade thanking our driver and coming up the walkway behind me; his gait just a bit slower.

He could be pissed all he wanted. I was well within my rights to be all up in my feelings. But even though I wanted to snatch her bald, I played my part. I knew the mission and I completed it.

Play nice.

Smile big.

Laugh at the right times.

Make Cade look good. Stand by his side.

Help other people see how amazing he was.

If I do say so myself, I was fucking fantastic tonight. To his credit, Cade didn't leave my side. As soon as the snide little Sylvia Martin made her comment and rushed off, we were approached by a beautiful dark-skinned woman. The wife of Stefano Indellicati. She introduced herself as Adele… just Adele. She didn't go for all that pomp and circumstance. Her words, not mine.

Cade greeted her warmly and introduced me. A huge smile came over her face and she leaned in slightly. "So, you're the one Cade always had to rush home to. Good, because that means Stefano's taken to coming home once they finish meetings or calls or whatever. It's nice to finally meet you."

I'd looked over at Cade to see him smirking down at me. Maybe he thought since Adele knew about me, or knew of the theoretical me, that it would make up for that rude ass woman. Okay, so sue me... my frustration did go down a notch. When Adele's attractive husband walked over to us, I could feel Cade pull me closer to him.

Not that the man was paying me any attention. Based on how he was looking at his beautiful wife, he clearly only had eyes for her. Respect.

Although the night ended up being very good for Cade due to the connections he made, I couldn't help but feel eyes on me all night. When I'd look around, it was usually that damn Sylvia and a group of other women huddled together like a gaggle of geese. When it came time for us to leave, I almost ran out of that building, but not before Adele made me promise to go out to brunch with her and some of the other wives of the owners. She said they were like family and with how much Cade was working with her husband, she wanted to make sure I felt welcome.

Now we were home. Let me change that. Now that we were back at Cade's house, all I wanted to do was go to sleep. Alone.

Why am I mad at him?

I have no fucking clue.

But that woman and her snide comment and sly looks brought up all my insecurities about my role in Cade's life. It was enough to make me re-evaluate everything. How many other people would question why his late wife's best friend was the woman he was bringing to events? How many other people would look at us with disdain, as if were doing something wrong?

Opening the door to the house, I took off my heels as soon as I stepped inside. It was almost ten-thirty, and I was positive Lilly was asleep. I stepped into the family room and found Stacy lying down on the couch. I lightly tapped her shoulder, just enough not to startle her. I did my best to give her a smile. I'm not sure how well I did, but she was half-sleep, so it didn't matter in the long run.

"Oh, hi, Ms. James. I didn't expect you back so soon," the teen said, wiping her eyes and standing.

"We finished just a bit early. How was Lilly tonight?"

She gathered her backpack, placing it over her shoulder. "Perfect. She's always so easy to babysit."

"Good," Cade stepped into the room. "Thanks again, Stacy." Reaching into his pocket, he pulled out a wad of cash and handed it to the girl. "I'll watch from the door as you walk home."

He always did that when she watched Lilly for us. Maybe it was an added bit of security, and yes, she was almost a senior in high school, but that's what made Cade so different to me. The man was a protector. Stacy was part of our circle. She protected our daughter… his daughter, so Cade made sure to keep a watchful eye on her.

"Night, Stacy. Thank you again."

Once she stepped over the threshold, she waved. "You're welcome. Have a good night."

I refused to stick around, so I started making my way up the stairs. Yes, I was avoiding Cade. I didn't feel like examining the emotions coursing through me. During the entire ride home, I was silent, even as Cade tried to talk to me. He knew things weren't right. Not the type of man to let things linger,

I knew he'd be following me. Hashing it out was his thing and while I usually had no problem going toe-to-toe with him, I wasn't in a good head space tonight.

Maybe I'd been fooling myself, thinking we could make this work. Perhaps I'd been living a fantasy this whole time, wishing for a life that wasn't meant to be mine. Either way, I was done. It hurt too much to think I was a stand-in.

When would it be my turn?

When would I be picked first, above all others?

God, I was pathetic. I could feel the tears welling in my eyes and tried to wipe them away before they fell.

"Norah!"

My feet sped up, practically tripping up the stairs as I rushed to my bedroom. If I closed the door in his face, maybe he'd get the message. Not tonight. I could hear him coming up the steps behind me. I panicked, a loud squeak coming out as I tried to move faster than he did.

Just as I made it into the room and tried to close the door, he pressed his large hand against the wood, stopping it from slamming in his face. "What the fuck, Norah? We're slamming doors now?"

"Go away, Cade. I'm not in the mood."

He stepped inside the room, and I watched as he slowly closed the door. Cade stared at me for a moment, he shook his head and began to remove his bowtie. "Fine. You're pissed about something. I get it. But we don't shut each other out, Norah. That's not how we do things. If you're upset about something, we talk about it." Removing his tie, he then unbuttoned his shirt, pulling it free of his tuxedo pants.

I stood on the other side of the room, hands on my hips. "What are you doing?"

He smirked at me. "What does it look like? I'm getting ready for bed."

Was he crazy? This wasn't happening tonight. "No, you're not. Sleep in your own bed."

He sat down on the settee at the end of the bed, glancing over his shoulder. "This is my bed. My bed with you. We haven't slept apart since that first night and I'm sure as hell not starting tonight."

"I told you I'm not in the mood." I'd never slept next to him without having him inside me, making love to me, whispering words of seduction in my ear. No, he had to leave. If he didn't, I wasn't sure I'd be able to keep my resolve.

"You don't have to be in the mood. I can sleep next to you without fucking you, Norah, but I'll be damned if I sleep in a different bed unable to hold you in my arms." Standing, he removed the rest of his clothes, leaving only his black boxers. As he walked into the bathroom, I heard him brush his teeth. The whole time, I stood in that same spot, wondering what game he was playing.

When he came out of the bathroom, he glanced over at me, before lifting one eyebrow. “Need some help getting undressed?”

“No,” I practically yelled. “Okay, yes. Can you unzip my dress?”

“Of course.” When he stood behind me, I could feel his breath on my neck. “You were amazing tonight. I don’t know what I did to piss you off, but I wish you’d talk to me.” Unzipping my dress, he stepped back. “Anything else?”

“No. I’m fine.” Where was this anger toward him coming from? Maybe it was nothing and everything all at once. We’d started sleeping together a month ago, and being a full-blown relationship was everything I’d dreamed of. He was attentive, he brought me flowers, and watched my shows with me, even as he grumbled the whole time. He was nothing like I expected but everything I wanted and needed in my life.

Maybe that was the problem, I thought, looking over at Cade as he climbed into the bed. Had I been pining over my best friend's husband for all these years? I didn't think I had, but now I was questioning everything. When that woman made her snarky comment and gave me that disparaging look, that feeling of being a fraud came roaring back.

I wanted Cade to want to be with me because I was me. Not because I was Lilly's godmother or because his late wife said we should be together. He needed to choose me because of who I was and what I meant to him. When we're together, I want to be the only woman he thought about. Was that selfish of me? Probably. But no woman wants to feel like a second choice.

After brushing my teeth, I walked out of the bathroom, turning off the light behind me. Cade looked up from his phone to watch me.

"Are we gonna talk about what's wrong with you tonight?"

Taking a deep sigh, I looked at him. His chest was bare, his arms thick and muscular. His dark beard trimmed, and I knew what I had to do. I chose violence.

"I'm not anyone's second choice, Cade."

He reared up, his eyes spitting fire, and his brow creased. "What the fuck does that mean, Norah?"

"I know you had a whole life before me. A wife. A daughter. You were happy. Doesn't matter that I saw you first. You chose her and I'm happy for you. But it feels like we're just playing house to pass the time. That I'm here with you because it's convenient, not because I'm the one you chose."

There I said it. I was practically hyperventilating but I got the words out. Not gonna lie, I knew those four glasses of champagne gave me some liquid courage, but that's just how the cookie crumbles. Would I have told him how I felt without the alcohol? Maybe not tonight, but I knew these feelings were bubbling up inside me. That woman at the party only accelerated things. They had to come out or else I was going to lose my shit.

Cade flipped the covers and got out of the bed, stalking over to me. "You think I'm here with you because you're convenient?" When I said nothing, he grabbed my chin in one of his hands, forcing my face up to his. "Answer me."

"I don't know."

Sighing, he grabbed one of my hands and pressed it against his thickening member. "Do you think I'm this hot for you because I don't want you? That I haven't dreamt about you almost every night for too damn long to count? Do you know how many chances I've had to scratch my itch with other women? They're coming out of every nook and cranny. None of them were able to get a reaction out of me. None of them. Only you. Every time you strolled your sexy ass in this house, taking over as if you belonged here, torturing me with your scent. I wanted to fuck you over every surface in this house, but I held back, respecting your boundaries. No, baby. I don't want you because you're convenient. I want you because you've always been mine. I didn't see it all those years ago and I'd probably still be blind to what's between us if Rebecca had lived. But she's gone and I have a second chance. I'm not losing you because you can't see how much I want you. How much I need you in my life. If you want to be pissed at me because of some random woman questioning your role in my life, that's your choice. But while you're pissed at me, know that I'm still not going to let you go. I'm going to sleep in that bed next to you every fucking night. You're going to be pressed up against me as I hold you close, thanking my fucking stars that you want me just as much as I want you." Leaning down, he brushed a light kiss on my lips, neck, and shoulder. "Now, get your ass in that bed so I can fuck you to sleep."

My panties were wet. My nipples were hard. My channel clenched in need. Well, damn. Were we about to have make-up sex?

Chapter 19

Cade

Leaning down, I inhaled Norah's unique scent. I would do whatever was needed for her to understand that what we had was real. From the moment Sylvia made that snide comment earlier, I knew shit was going to hit the fan. I hadn't seen her in a while, but we ran in the same circles. She'd been to our house when Norah had been there. She'd attended Rebecca's funeral. I'm surprised Norah didn't remember her.

I didn't have to answer to Sylvia, or anyone else. My decisions were mine to make. My life was mine to live. Who I chose to live it with was no one's business but my own. If given a choice, I would choose Norah every single time. It didn't mean I forgot the life I'd had before, but this is the one I want now. She is the woman I need by my side in the future. She may need a little help getting caught up, but I had no doubt she wanted this life with me.

"Now, get your ass in that bed so I can fuck you to sleep." Smacking her on the ass, I smiled when she jumped.

"That hurt." Her bottom lip poked out and she rubbed her backside.

"That's for continuing to doubt me. To doubt us. If I have to fuck you so hard every night that you can't think straight the next day, that's what I'll do. I'm happy with what we have. I want to build a future with you, Norah. Stop letting other people make you question what we have. What we're building."

Since she wasn't moving fast enough for me, I bent down, scooping her up in my arms and placing her down on the bed.

"Cade, I'm trying."

"Fucking try harder." Her eyes went wide at my tone. I stood up from the bed, closed my eyes, and took a few deep breaths. I wasn't angry at her, but I also didn't appreciate how much she pulled back from the idea of us. Looking down at Norah, I felt the question bubble up to the surface. "Are you ashamed to be with me?"

"No," she practically yelled. Getting up on her knees, she placed her hands on my chest. "I would never be ashamed of you. Everything about you is perfect. You're a good man. A great father. An amazing lover. I couldn't ask for anyone better."

Running a finger down her jaw, I couldn't help the feeling inside me. "I'm so lucky to have you."

She shook her head. Of course, even in this moment, she had to be stubborn. "I'm the lucky one. You look at me every day and tell me I'm beautiful. Even when I wake up with my bonnet all twisted and sleep in my eyes." She paused, laughing. "Trust me, every woman wants to hear that in the morning. You've opened your life to me and allowed me to step inside. You share your child with me, even though you don't have to."

Gripping her around the waist, I interrupted her speech. "I didn't have a choice. You are Lilly's second mother. You're the one who brought laughter into this house again. You brought me back from the brink of turning into the type of man I don't ever want to be." Hooking my hands in her underwear, I began to shift them down her body. "Now, as I said, I need you naked and ready for me, because I need to be inside you."

I'd already removed my briefs, so my thick cock was hard and ready to join the party. She allowed me to remove her panties by lifting each leg as I slid the material down her body. She had on a t-shirt, which I removed just as quickly. Once she was bare, I pressed her back on the bed. "I want to touch and taste and lick every part of your body tonight."

"I'm all yours," she whispered.

Pausing, I leaned up on my elbows and stared at her. "Are you, Norah? Because I'm tired of playing these games. I want you all in with me. I know who I want and that's you, but I need you with me." Nodding, she lifted her head to kiss me, but I pulled back. "I need you to use your words. I don't want there to be any confusion. I thought we were done questioning what we mean to each other."

"We are, Cade. I'm done questioning if you want me. I know where I belong."

Bumping her entrance with my dick, I dipped my head and took her beaded nipple into my mouth. "And where is that?"

"Right here. With you," she murmured as I trailed one hand down her body. My fingers met her wet folds and I toyed with the hardened nub between her thighs. Her scent increased as she squirmed beneath me. The tip of one finger pressed inside her hot sheath. "Cade," she moaned in response to my touch.

"What?" I watched her legs widen as my thick finger slid further inside her body. Looking between her legs, I watched my digit as it exited her body, the skin slick and wet from her fluids. It was a beautiful sight.

"Please."

I pressed my fingers deeper as her legs widened. Using my thumb, I rubbed it against her clit. Norah's body seized in pleasure, her breathing sped up, and her fingers clawed at my bare skin. My baby was about to explode. Just as she was about to fall off the cliff, I shifted, placing my mouth against her pussy. Diving face first into her puffy mound with my tongue leading the way, nothing else mattered but tasting her.

Ambrosia.

Spreading her toned legs as wide as they could go, all I cared about was giving her pleasure. I wanted her to scream my name, grab my head, pull me closer, and force me to give her what she needed. This was my woman and everything I did was for her.

Sucking her clit, I listened for that sound I loved so much. That keening wail that told me she was mine. The one that told me my actions brought her to this place. I grabbed the back of her thighs, pushed her legs back, devouring her with my lips and tongue. I could do this every single night. Hell, I'd done it every night since the first moment she allowed me in her bed. Something about her taste made me lose my fucking mind. Nothing would ever take her away from me. More. I wanted more of her. I needed it.

"Cade. Please. Cade. Yes. Fuck," she chanted above me.

My dick was throbbing with need. I lifted my head at the sound of her plea. Then, wiping my mouth, I quickly shifted my body so that my dick was pressed against her. Norah's hands reached out to me.

"Please, Cade. I need you."

"Damn, baby. I love to hear you beg," I growled, pressing inside her. She was always such a tight fit. No matter how many times I claimed her this way, each time felt like the first. Her body always squeezed me so good, pulling me inside as if she never wanted to let me go. A hiss escaped my lips as I thrust inside her slowly. "Look at me," I demanded when she closed her eyes. "I need you to see me. I need you to be here with me."

She nodded. "Yes. I'm here. I see you, Cade."

When I reached as deep as I could, I stopped before leaning down to kiss her softly. "Don't leave me," I begged. The words felt torn from my throat, but I meant them. Losing her would take me to a place I wouldn't come back from.

"Never. I'll never leave you."

I pulled back and thrust inside again, reveling in the sensation of being with her. Tonight started out amazing, then almost turned to shit, but ended in the best way possible. With me inside my woman as she writhed underneath me.

This is what I'd been dreaming about all night, being inside her. No matter what happened, even if the event had been a bust, sliding inside her slick channel was the only thing I needed. Norah's body accepted me like it was welcoming me home. Maybe because this is where I belonged. Her hands played in my hair before rubbing along my back, my sides, and my arms.

"Yes, Cade."

Thrusting harder, I pressed her legs up higher, bringing her knees almost to her ears. I couldn't get deep enough. I wanted to imprint on her body, so that she knew that she belonged to me, that I belonged to her. Staring down at her, I wanted to share how I truly felt, but I didn't think she was ready just yet. It felt like she was sucking me inside, tightening and molding around me.

She was a perfect fucking fit.

Nothing had ever felt this good, and I meant that shit. Nothing.

To think, she would have tried to go to bed without letting me have her like this. "Don't ever hold back from me. We don't go to bed upset. We talk it out or we fuck it out. Whatever it takes. Do you hear me?" Her eyes were glazed over in ecstasy, which is what I wanted to see. I needed to see. But I still needed her to understand what the fuck I was saying. "We work our shit out, Norah. I can't take it when you're upset with me. I can't accept that," I could hear myself almost pleading with her and got angry all over again. I needed her to believe in me, in us.

"Yes. Okay. I'm sorry. I'm sorry," she whimpered.

Every stroke inside her body was a promise. Every time I tapped her cervix, it was a vow to build a future together. Lilly would not be an only child. I wanted to give her a little brother and a little sister. Every kiss was meant to let Norah know what was in my heart, even if she didn't hear the message. Every time I came inside her, I recommitted myself to her and the life we were building with each other.

I could feel her channel clenching around me as I pounded inside her body even harder. Folding her almost in half, I wrapped my arms underneath her glistening form, grabbing her lush ass in my palms. Squeezing her flesh, I focused on hitting the spot that made my baby gush. She was perfect for me. When we were in bed together, Norah gave me everything she had. Her body was mine. The breathy moans she released were mine. Even the tears that fell from her eyes as her orgasm rushed through her body belonged to me.

As her body began to shake, I moved one hand from her ass and braced it against the headboard. “That’s it, baby. Come for me. Give Daddy what he needs.”

“Mmmm hmmm. Yes. I’m—I’m…”

“Fuck, Norah. You’re squeezing me so tight. That right there is what I need,” I said as her back arched and she let out that beautiful sound I loved to hear.

That was all the motivation I needed. Grinding harder and deeper, I wanted to prolong her orgasm because I knew it would make mine even better. Releasing inside her every night like this, I was surprised we hadn’t already made a miracle. I smiled down at her as I felt her explode around me. I had no doubt that I would be getting my wish soon.

Norah James would be my wife one day soon, she just didn't know it yet.

At that thought, I felt my body seize up as I allowed myself to let go. My hips jerked a few times as I focused on getting every bit of my release inside her. I didn't want any to escape. Primal need filled me as I pictured her pregnant with my child.

Fuck, it was a beautiful sight.

Rolling to the side, I pulled her tight against me. When Norah came to live in the house full-time, I had no idea things would be like this between the two of us. But this feeling, the happiness, the peace I felt, was unlike anything I'd anticipated.

Now that we'd had our first fight as a couple, and the best make-up sex on this side of the Mississippi, I only hoped nothing else would happen to make her doubt what we had. Even if it did, I would fight every single day to hold on to her and the life we'd built.

Chapter 20

Norah

We were lounging on the couch, Lilly between us, as we relaxed after returning from the park. "Lilly, you're getting better every time. Pretty soon, I won't be able to keep up with you."

"Thanks, auntie Norah. Can we have ice cream tonight after dinner?"

The doorbell rang and Cade got up from the couch and walked to the front of the house. Pretty soon, she heard voices coming through. I recognized the woman's voice, and my entire body froze like a deer in headlights.

Rebecca's mother.

What the fuck

"Lilly, your grandmother's here," Cade called out.

I held my breath as the scene unfolded in front of me. I'd always gotten along with Mrs. Spencer, but I had no idea how to respond to her today. Did I act as if everything was still the same? I mean, I'd spent just as much time at her house as my own. As the silver-haired woman walked in, her eyes landed on Lilly first.

"Lilly! You've gotten so big. I've missed you." Mrs. Spencer opened her arms to her granddaughter, gathering the little girl close. "How's school going? Are you ready for the summer?"

I couldn't help but smile at their interaction. Cade walked behind them before coming to stand next to me. When he moved to take my hand, I shifted away. I wasn't rejecting him, but from the look in his eyes, you wouldn't know it. It was difficult to understand why I was feeling this way. Still, he had to know that this wasn't the best way to let his ex-mother-in-law know that he'd moved on and started a new relationship.

"Hi, Mrs. Spencer," I finally called out.

Lifting her head, she smiled at me. Then taking note of how close Cade and I were standing, her head tilted as she looked between us. For a moment, I saw her lips thin, and her eyes squinted in what appeared to be anger. Then the look was gone, and she pasted a smile on her face. "Hey, Norah. It's good to see you again. How have you been?"

So, maybe this wouldn't be as painful as I thought. "I'm okay. Still adjusting."

The older woman nodded. "Hmmm. Yes, aren't we all. It's still hard to believe I can't pick up the phone and call her."

"Me too." I could hear the warble in my voice. Then, clearing my throat, I smiled for the sake of Lilly, who was watching us with curious eyes. "Is Mr. Spencer coming as well?"

Shaking her head, she walked further into the room. "Not today. He's tired from the drive. I told him I'd just do a quick pop-up to see this little lady here, and then I'd be back. We're here for the next two weeks, so there's going to be plenty of time for us to drive you both crazy."

"Grandma, do you want to see my drawings? I made some of mommy."

Mrs. Spencer nodded at Lilly. "I sure do. Lead the way." Placing her purse on a chair, she allowed herself to be pulled into the family room. Before she left, she paused for a moment to look at me and Cade. "I hope I didn't interrupt anything. Maybe I should have called before I arrived."

"No. You didn't interrupt anything," Cade responded for us. I glanced at him and saw that his brow was still furrowed, probably in frustration with me. But I didn't care if he was upset. This was not the way to tell Mrs.

Spencer that he and I were in a relationship… or whatever this was.

"Good. Good." She patted my arm and smiled at me. A genuine smile this time. "It really is good to see you again, Norah."

"Yes, ma'am. I'm glad you're here. I know Lilly is so happy that she can spend time with you."

As Cade and I watched the two of them walk away, I opened my mouth to broach the subject, but he beat me to it.

"What the fuck, Norah?"

I shrugged. "I'm not telling her that way. She deserves more respect than that. I was her daughter's best friend for most of my life."

He turned to look down at me, crossing his large arms over his chest. "Is this how it's going to be all the time? You're just going to be too scared and ashamed to tell people we're together? I get it. Behind closed doors, we can be a couple, pretend to be a family. But in public, you pull away from me. Deny what we are to each other?"

Shaking my head, I stepped away. How dare he? "I never said that. She's your late wife's mother. She's a woman who invited me into her home. I stood next to her daughter when she married you, pledged her life to you while you did the same. But now that she's gone, I just happen to slide into the spot in your life she left vacant?" My voice was low because I didn't want Mrs. Spencer to hear us, but my clipped tone made my displeasure known. "Don't be cruel to a woman still dealing with the loss of her only child. That's not fair to her. You can frown down at me all you want, but it won't change how I feel."

Sighing, I looked at him one last time. "You've asked me to accept what we have, and I do. I never want to be without you again. I know that now. But I won't hurt the people who've meant so much to me over the years. You can't ask me to do that."

Cade ran a hand down his face as he took a deep breath. "Norah." He said my name as if it were a plea.

On the one hand, I knew what he was going through, but I had to do this my way. It was the only way I could truly feel comfortable. "Just let me tell her on my own. I'm not going to throw our relationship in her face."

"I don't like it. She knows I loved her daughter. Elizabeth is here to see her granddaughter. Me being in a relationship with you shouldn't matter."

And the fact that he called her Elizabeth while I still called her Mrs. Spencer told me everything I needed to know. His relationship with Rebecca's mother was on a different level than mine. I also knew that I was probably giving her more leverage over my life, and Cade's life, than was warranted. At thirty-one years old, not even my own mother could tell me how to live my life. Glancing over my shoulder, I mumbled. "It shouldn't, but it does." Then, turning back to him, I tried again. "Give me today."

"Fine. You have three hours. I'm not going to spend the entire day not touching you or kissing you. Don't try to hide me, Norah. That's not something I'm okay with. It's time for you to decide if you want this relationship more than you fear what others will say about us."

Nodding at his words, I turned and walked into the family room where Mrs. Spencer… Elizabeth and Lilly were sitting on the couch looking at drawings. "She's really good," I interjected. "Every day, she has a new picture for us."

Lifting her gaze to mine, Elizabeth nodded. "She gets it from her mother." She lifted a finger to wipe below her eyes. I'm sure seeing her granddaughter brought up so many emotions. When she glanced up at me, I saw the look in her eyes and braced myself for what she would say next. "Cade told me he asked you to come back and live with the two of them. He said he was having a hard time with Lilly. You've been here about five months now?"

Nodding, I tried to stop my hands from shaking. Maybe this was the actual test of how I felt about Cade. Was I ashamed of the relationship we were building? Did I still worry people would think what we were doing was inappropriate? Of course, it wasn't, but that didn't stop the feeling of doubt coursing through my veins.

"Yes, just about five months now. I wasn't sure how it would work out. My life was in Baltimore for so many years, but with my job, I can work from anywhere."

Elizabeth looked down at Lilly, who was drawing another picture for them. "She seems to be doing much better. Her beautiful smiles show up more. When we're on our weekly video calls, she talks about her mom without going silent. She'll just bring up a story or a fact about her mother that I never thought she knew."

Capturing the older woman's gaze, I sat a little taller. Maybe this was my moment. "I want to make sure she knows all the things about Rebecca that will help her feel connected to her mother. All the memories I have from the time we were seven years old. I want to share them with Lilly, so she knows just how amazing her mother was. For as long as I'm around, she'll never forget her mother. Lilly will know the amazing person I grew up with, laughed with, cried with. It's important that she knows who her mother truly was."

For a moment, the room was silent, other than the mumblings of Lilly as she talked to herself while drawing.

"How long do you plan to stay?"

Stay in the house? Stay around Lilly? Stay where…? I wasn't sure which question she was asking, so I scrambled for the correct response.

The older woman's eyebrows raised as she looked at me with a question on her face.

"Stay?" I repeated.

After staring at me for a few seconds, she smirked before continuing. "I know the plan was for you to stay here with Cade and Lilly for six months and that time is almost up. Will you be leaving? Going back to Baltimore and the life you built there?"

I didn't have an answer for her. Only because I hadn't really fleshed out the plan of what would happen. Cade assumed I would be here for good. He'd said multiple times that this was my home, that this was *our home.* I didn't want to leave him or Lilly, but if we were to try and make a go of it, could I live in this house? Eventually, he'd want to go back to his own bedroom. Could I make love to him in the same bed where he'd slept with Rebecca? Those answers would have to come another day, but I did know one thing.

"I'm not leaving Lilly. I love her as if she were my own daughter. Rebecca and I talked about what would happen after… after…" pausing, I took a moment to pull myself together. "We talked about what she wanted for Lilly's future. I plan to give that to her."

Nodding, she stared at me silently, with eyes that reminded me of my best friend. "So, you're staying for the long haul. With Lilly?"

"Yes."

"With Cade?"

There was no malice in her voice, but I knew what she was asking. She'd have to be blind to not see how we interacted with each other in just those few minutes when she arrived. "Would it concern you if I said yes?"

Holding my breath, I waited for her to respond. Instead, she looked around the house, her eyes landing on the family picture of Cade, Rebecca, and Lilly.

"Should I be concerned, Norah?"

I shook my head. "No."

"My daughter loved her husband."

Nodding, I agreed. "She did, and he loved her. Still does. That won't change. She'll always be in his heart. She's the mother of his child. They built a life together."

Elizabeth ran her hand down the back of Lilly's head. "Lilly? Can you ask your dad to help you get a glass of juice for your grandmother?"

"Yes, Grandma. I'll be back!"

Once she left the room, Elizabeth turned back to me. "I wasn't sure about Rebecca's plan when she first mentioned it to me."

My jaw dropped. Was Rebecca manipulating everyone this entire time? "Rebecca's plan?"

The other woman nodded. "She talked to me about her need to make sure Cade and Lilly were taken care of. She also said she had some… regrets… about how things happened years ago. I'm not sure what she meant by that, she never told me the whole story. Do you know what she meant by regrets?"

Still in a state of semi-shock, I nodded. "Yes, I do."

Laughing, Elizabeth tilted her head back. "Robert told me that our daughter knew what she was doing. That it wasn't up to us, but it was hard to accept what she felt was the right thing. When you left and only returned on the weekends to see Lilly, I thought the plan had failed since you were too focused on your own life to try and create a new one as a mother to a child who wasn't yours." Her eyes looked calculating, as if assessing me. "To fall in love with a man who had been in love with someone else."

Standing quickly from the chair, I felt the need to walk away and deny her words. I didn't want to have this conversation with her. The accusations would come and that would be too difficult for me to hear. "No. I mean, yes. I love Lilly. But Cade and I… um… we're…"

Rising from the couch, Elizabeth walked over to me. She grabbed me by the arms, "It's okay, Norah. I know you love Lilly. I know you loved my daughter like a sister. You were sisters in every way that counts, other than parentage. And I know you love Cade." She stared into my eyes. "Oh, you haven't told him yet?"

Dropping my head in defeat, a pained whisper broke free. "No."

Releasing my arms from her grasp, she stepped back. "This won't do at all. It's time you two stop fighting this thing between you. This is now your life to live. Stop waiting for approval, or rejection. If you're waiting for my blessing, which you shouldn't be, you have it. It's okay for you to have happiness, even if Rebecca isn't here to enjoy it with you." Patting me on the hand, she walked away, leaving me alone with my thoughts.

Well, damn. Seems like I'm the only one who didn't know what Rebecca had planned for me and my future. As I stood by myself thinking of everything that had happened in the last year and a-half, I couldn't help the laughter bubbling up. Even in death, my best friend was bossy as hell. "Fine, Rebecca. Message received."

Chapter 21

Norah

The next day, after Cade kissed me goodbye and Lilly was off to school, I quickly dressed. Then, dialing the number of the one person I needed to speak with today, I waited for her to pick up.

"Hello, baby."

"Hi, Momma. You busy?" I prayed she had time for me today.

"I'm just fiddling around the house. What's up?"

"I'm on the way to you. I need to talk. See you in about twenty minutes."

I heard her sigh on the other line. "I figured this moment was coming soon. I'll be here. You hungry?"

This woman was always trying to feed me. Maybe that's why she and Cade got along so well. "For your cooking? Always." We hung up and I drove the familiar route to my mother's home. This situation between Cade and I needed to be resolved. It seemed that I was the only one keeping us apart. He was right, I couldn't be half-in. If we were going to be together, then I needed to jump in with both feet.

Last night, as we made love—in my bedroom—I almost said the words that would change everything.

Did I love him? Yes.

He made me feel special, unique, loved, and cared for. We slept together every night. When we made love, I felt that not only was my life falling into place, but that he was the only one who could have put all the pieces back together. He whispered seductive words in my ear, told me how beautiful I was every day.

Passing each other in the hallway as we simply lived our lives, he'd reach out and touch me, grabbing my hand in his. He'd even stop me for a quick kiss. Not enough to get something started, but just what I needed to let me know he was thinking of me, that I was on his mind.

That's not to say the man didn't drive me crazy, because he did. He wanted to control the world around him, which included me and Lilly. To him, our safety was the only thing that mattered. The slightest headache or sniffle had him ready to take us to every specialist in the DC metro area. Not that I didn't understand, because I did. He wasn't willing to risk losing anyone else. I felt the same way.

Pulling up to my mother's house, it took less than a minute to park and walk inside the door. "Something smells good," I called out.

"Hey honey. I'm in the kitchen."

Breakfast was my favorite meal of the day, and my mother had never forgotten. French toast, bacon, and eggs were laid out on multiple platters. As my mother grabbed some juice from the fridge, I sat at the breakfast nook. “Mom, you didn’t have to make all this.”

She gave me an indulgent smile. “You have no idea how long I’ve been waiting for this conversation. I’m not letting you leave without talking things out. And to do that, we need food.”

Snagging a slice of bacon, I began eating. “What do you mean, you’ve been waiting for this conversation? I just realized this morning that I needed to talk to you.”

She came and sat next to me as she began making a plate of food for herself. “This is about Cade, right? Your feelings for him and his for you?” At the look I gave her, she laughed. “Honey, I’ve lived a whole life, and then some. Trust me, I knew this day was coming. So, what are you struggling with?"

Not sure where to start, I began with the end. "I'm in love with him." Just saying the words made something squeeze inside me. Even though it was scary to finally put the words out there, it also felt good to share it with my mother. She knew what happened all those years ago, even if it took me a while to tell her. When I picked up and left for Baltimore when Rebecca became pregnant, she was the only one who had any inkling of the real reason.

I was running.

Hiding from my emotions and feeling like the worst friend ever.

"I know you do," she smirked.

That's it? "What do you mean, you know I do?"

Wiping her hands and mouth with a napkin, she turned to look at me. "I know you love him because I know my child. I also know that you've probably been fighting it this entire time, telling yourself that you didn't deserve to find happiness after your friend died. Norah, love doesn't care about what makes sense. Love is blind to the foibles of humans. The one person you think you don't have the right to love, is the one person meant for you. Did I ever tell you about when I first met your father?"

I nodded. "Yeah. You told me how the two of you met in high school. You always told me he was the finest boy on campus."

Laughing for a moment, she looked at me. "Yes, he sure was. But did I tell you that when we met, he had a girlfriend, and I was talking to a boy everyone thought was perfect for me?" When I shook my head, she continued. "Your father and I never ran in the same circles. He was a jock. I was quiet as a mouse, always with my nose in a book. He was fine alright, but I never thought he was interested in me. Plus, his girlfriend at the time, was the Queen Bee. They were a power couple."

I'd never heard this version of the story, so now I was intrigued. When my mom paused, I pressed. "What happened."

"I was clumsy. Wasn't paying attention and bumped into your dad and his girlfriend in the hallway when we changed classes. I made her drop her books and I dropped mine also, but that didn't matter to her. She went all the way off. It was so embarrassing. But in the mess, your father kneeled to help me grab my stuff from the ground. Not hers. Mine. It was something about that moment, our eyes catching as we both tried to ignore the ravings of his girlfriend, that I knew."

I listened with bated breath; my eyes were wide with curiosity. "Knew what?"

She gave me a side-eye and a tiny smile. "That I would have him. I wanted him to be mine and his girlfriend wasn't going to stand in my way. To this day, I don't think he understands just how much I wanted him. And that's what you have to do."

I rolled my eyes and took a sip of my juice. "Mom, this isn't high school."

My mom shook her head then grabbed my hand. "Listen to me. I know it's not high school, but it's time for you to stop hiding behind what others expect of you. I hid my face in books because I didn't see my value. Being invisible was best for me because if people saw me, they might judge me. We weren't rich. My clothes weren't the best. I wasn't light skinned with long, permed hair. I was dark-skinned, with natural hair, and wore clothes that were purchased at the discount store. But here's the part you're not connecting… that boy, your father, he saw me. He didn't care that other people never thought we should be together. When we walked together, he grabbed my hand and kissed me right in front of everyone else. His focus was on me and making me happy. Letting me know that I was his priority, and he didn't care what others thought. Even though I'd made a vow that I would have him, I still had to accept that his feelings for me were just as real, that he wanted me just as much. Thirty-five years later, we've built a life, a home, a family, that has been a blessing to me every single day."

I'd never heard any of this and it threw me for a loop. "Mom, I never knew you felt that way when you met Dad."

"No, you didn't. It seems like someone else's story. I don't even recognize the young girl I was back then. Hiding from the world. Not allowing myself to go after what I wanted. Even letting others dictate if I was worthy of love from the one person who made me feel complete." She stood up from the chair and took her empty plate to the sink. "Does that remind you of anyone?"

I looked away, smirking. Smart lady. "I see what you did there." Sighing, I dropped my gaze for a moment. "I love him. I love his daughter. We've started to build something together, but I keep pulling away."

"What does he say when you do that?"

I thought of his words and winced. "That I need to be all in, that he doesn't care about what others think, we know what feels right." As I looked across the kitchen at my beautiful, confident mother, I still couldn't believe people thought she didn't deserve to be with my father. "There was never anything between Cade and I when Rebecca was alive."

She nodded at me. "I know that, too."

"How?" I was truly curious, because with how hot and heavy we'd been going, it was like we'd been in a relationship for years, not just a couple months.

"Because you had too much respect for Rebecca. And you have too much respect for yourself." Grabbing my hand, she smiled at me. "Norah, it's okay to find your happiness. This world will judge you no matter what. You can do the right thing every single time and someone will find fault. What you feel for Cade isn't wrong and you have to come to grips with that. If you don't figure this out for yourself, you're going to lose that man. Is that what you want? For someone else to be standing by his side, raising his child, while you stand back and wish it were you? Again?"

I pulled back at the picture she painted in her head. "Mom, Rebecca left me a letter. Apparently, she had it delivered to Cade for him to give it to me. It was so crazy to read her words to me. She told me she wanted me to open myself to love. I think she's been pulling the strings this entire time."

My mom laughed. "You might be right. You know I talk to Elizabeth every couple of weeks or so. She told me Rebecca was trying to fix things for everyone even while she was sick. Is that true?"

"It's true."

"Did she fix things for you?"

Thinking about the eighteen months, I couldn't help but smile. "She tried."

"What didn't work?"

Closing my eyes, I realized exactly what… or who… the problem was. "She didn't count on me being just as stubborn as she was." Gathering my phone and keys, I hopped out of the chair and went to kiss my mom on the cheek. "I have to go. Something important I need to do."

Laughter followed me. "It's about time. Oh, Elizabeth and I want a June wedding and another grandchild to spoil."

If everything went the way I wanted, they'd get their wish. Thinking of all the pieces that I had to put in place, I called Cade's office.

When Mildred picked up, the first part of the plan came together.

This was it. I was going after what I wanted. I'd done all the right things, but I was still holding back, wasting my life trying to be someone else. A person that no one else expected of me, but myself. What I felt for Cade was real. When he held me in his arms at night and I inhaled his scent, I felt safe. I felt loved, even if he hadn't said the words.

Then again, why would he? Every time he opened himself to me, my mind started thinking of all the reasons we shouldn't be together. It had been a constant push-pull. If this was unfair to anyone, it was Cade.

Pulling up to the house… our house, I glanced at the time displayed on my phone. I had one hour to get to Cade's office. Of course, he would never expect what was about to happen, but I knew it was time for me to finally claim the man I wanted.

We didn't need anyone else's blessing, but he needed to hear me say the words. Cade wanted me, all of me, without hesitation or reservation. It was time to let him know exactly how I felt in return. Just thinking about Cade made me think of my favorite bible quote.

Love is patient, love is kind. It does not envy, it does not boast, it is not proud. It does not dishonor others, it is not self-seeking, it is not easily angered, it keeps no record of wrongs. Love does not delight in evil but rejoices with the truth. It always protects, always trusts, always hopes, always perseveres.

That was me and Cade, or at least how I pictured us. We'd both gone through hell and back during these past few years, but we persevered. We loved strongly and it burns brighter every single day. I would no longer deny what I felt.

Now it was time to show him.

Chapter 22

Cade

I was still thinking about yesterday, and Rebecca's mother coming to the house. It hadn't been a surprise, but I can admit that I held that information from Norah. With the way she'd been feeling, I felt she needed to be jarred into action. I'd been too indulgent with her, allowing her to dictate the pace of our relationship. I knew seeing Elizabeth would cause Norah to do one of two things… fight for us and the life we were building or run away.

As it turned out, she'd done neither.

Even after their talk in the family room, where I knew the subject of our relationship came up—I'd planned it with Elizabeth after all—Norah was still skittish. She'd stopped pulling away from me when I touched her hand

and wrapped my arm around her waist, but I could tell she was still somewhat uncomfortable.

When we went to bed that night, she'd tried to hold back from me, but I wasn't allowing that shit to happen either. I made sure Norah knew that trying to hide from me wasn't going to work.

Looking at my watch, I saw that only twenty minutes had passed. It felt like two hours. I'd just finished a call with Overwatch Security about some ads they wanted to place in the international airports. Savvy business move. I was still thankful every day that I'd partnered with them. Plus, I liked the men who ran the company. They were family men. Mission-oriented. Former military. My kind of people.

Mildred knocked on the door, interrupting his thoughts. "I'm heading out for an appointment. I'll be back tomorrow."

"Everything okay?" I knew it wasn't always the right thing to ask your employees, especially if they were dealing with personal issues, but Mildred had been with me for years. If something was going on with her, I wanted to know.

She waved me off. "Yes, everything's fine. Just some things I need to take care of. See you tomorrow."

As she walked out, I thought about heading home myself. But, with everything so up in the air with Norah, I didn't feel like being in the office. Instead, I wanted to be wrapped up in her arms, her body close to mine. It had been a long time since I felt this intense need for someone. Nothing against Rebecca, but the depth of my feelings for Norah… well, let's just say, what I felt for her was different.

It hurt like hell that she was still pushing me away. I was trying to understand, but it was hard. I'd given up so much of my life to do what was expected of me. I married the woman who loved me more than her own life, had a beautiful little girl, and built the picture-perfect life. Did it matter that I hadn't craved her the way I do Norah? No. Because I gave her every piece of me that I could give her at the time. It just so happens, that I'm now able to provide Norah with more.

A knock sounded on my door, breaking through my musings. "Come in." Expecting it to be one of my employees, I didn't bother looking up. "Yes?"

"I was wondering if you had time for an early lunch."

My head lifted at the first word that left her mouth. "Norah? Baby, what are you doing here?" I watched her lock my office door. She had on a blue wraparound dress. It was the one I loved removing from her body with just the pull of a piece of cloth that functioned as the tie around her waist. It was the one thing keeping her luscious body hidden from view. I stood from my chair and made my way around my desk. "Is everything okay? Why are you…?"

"I love you."

Her words stopped me in my tracks. My eyes bulged and my heart stuttered. That feeling people have when their world tilts on its axis? I was feeling all of that and more.

"What did you say?"

Her smile was like a beacon of light, blinding me as I tried to fight through. Needing to be closer, I reached out and grabbed one of her hands, pulling her close. I didn't even recognize my voice when I spoke. "Tell me again."

Lifting one hand, she cradled my jaw. Her other hand rested on top of mine as I gripped her waist tight. "I love you, Cade."

Eyes closing, I sent up a silent prayer of thanks. "I didn't think I'd ever hear you say those words. I've been waiting for you…"

"I know and I'm sorry for that. I've been in love with you for… well, it's been a while. But I'm tired of holding back. You and Lilly mean everything to me. You're my life. My place is by your side."

Tightening my hold on her, I brought her body flush with mine. "What about your concerns? Other people may not understand at first."

She nodded and my disappointment flared. For once, I wanted her to choose me. To choose us. Fuck everyone else if they didn't understand what was happening between us. The people closest to us knew the deal. They understood how everything went down. Yet, all they cared about was our happiness. I needed Norah to focus on that also.

She stepped back from me, my hand reaching out to keep her close. Shaking her head, her hands went to the belt of her dress… then she pulled. My dick thickened in my jeans as I stood in front of her. Every inch of her skin called out to me.

"Baby?"

"Yes, Cade." The dress fell from her shoulders, landing on the floor at her feet.

She wore a purple satin bra with matching panties. It didn't matter to me what she had on. Hell, white cotton would have had the same effect on me. I wanted to slide inside her body. I craved her scent. Needed her pussy attached to my mouth as she screamed and moaned my name.

"What are you doing, Norah?"

Unhooking her bra, she flung it to the side. "I'm here to tell you that I'm not going anywhere. I spent so much time waiting for a second chance, but there was always some reason to not feel good enough for you, for this life. It was hard at the end of the day, loving you, being with you, wanting you to see the real me, that I didn't recognize that you already did. You saw me, Norah, not a replacement. You came to my bed every night and gave every bit of yourself. You found comfort in my arms and yet, I still tried to deny you. Deny us."

I heard her words, but I was still focused on her movements. Grabbing her underwear, she slid them down those long brown legs, and I almost reached out to her. She was teasing the fuck out of me and all I wanted was to be inside her.

"Cade, you are the man I want. You're the man I love. And if you'll have me, we can build a life together. Have a family with Lilly."

"I want more babies," the words slipped out, but I knew that I meant them. I wanted Norah pregnant with my child. But, first, I needed to get a ring on her finger so I could lock her ass down.

Tilting her head, she smiled, before taking a step closer to me. “Babies? As in more than one?”

Nodding, I grabbed her tight and began walking back toward the couch against the wall. My office was filled with all the executive accoutrements it needed to impress my clients. That meant a full-size sofa, a single wing-back chair, and a coffee table. Today, that couch would be the place I’d fuck my woman into oblivion.

“I want as many babies as you want to give me.”

As I looked down at her watching me, I couldn’t believe how lucky I was. Some men have trouble finding happiness once. In my life, I’ve loved only two women, one of whom was in my arms.

“I’m here to say I’m sorry for making you wait. For questioning who I am to you. Mildred is gone for the day. Your outer office door is locked, and your woman is standing naked in front of you. So, what are you going to do about that, Mr. Donovan?"

Turning, I sat down on the couch before bringing her onto my lap, her legs spread wide as she straddled me. "I'm going to give you what you're asking for." I grabbed her around the back of the neck as I pulled her face closer to mine. Kissing her soft lips, I heard and felt her moan. Her lower body began to shift and twist as she ground into my hard cock. As she broke away and pulled back, I looked into her eyes. "I love you, Norah. I will be faithful. I will come back to you every night. You are my light, guiding me home."

She nodded, wiping away the wetness that filled her eyes at my words. I wasn't trying to make her sad, but I needed her to understand my feelings for her. I wanted to taste her lips every morning and night.

Her hands were at my waistband, undoing my belt buckle, pulling my shirt out from my pants, freeing my cock. “You want this dick, baby?”

Nodding, she lifted her body, positioning her slick channel over my burgeoning member. “Yes.”

Fuck, I wanted her touch. I wanted to claim her. I wanted to never be separated from her again. Grabbing her hips, I controlled the pace as I pulled her down, breaching her center. We both hissed at the feeling. She tried to press further, but I held her still. “No. You came to me wanting to play, so I get to control the game.”

“Cade. Please,” she whined.

“Beg me for more,” I demanded.

“Please, baby. I need you inside me. Stop making me wait.”

I chuckled. “Demanding, aren’t we?”

Nodding, she cradled my face in her hands before planting a soft kiss on my lips. "I need you."

Finally acquiescing, I bit her bottom lip hard and surged inside her in one thrust. "Fuck," I yelled.

"Cade," Norah screamed as she felt the full brunt of my entry.

Groaning at the slick, tight heat of her pussy, I sunk into the pleasure she was giving me. No matter how many times I claimed her, her body welcomed me as if it were the first time. Determined to bring her to the brink, I pushed inside her body as I held her bottom half still. Her fingers clutched my shoulders as she urged me on with soft cries and whimpers that were music to my ears. With those sweet pleas releasing from her mouth, I had no choice but to go deeper, needing to find that soft spot inside her that always made her shake and quiver.

“Fuck! Cade. Yes,” she chanted.

“There you go, baby. Just like that.”

She leaned forward to kiss me, and I could feel her begin to clench around my hard shaft still pounding inside her. "Norah, give it to me. You feel so good wrapped around my dick.” My baby loved it when I talked dirty to her. Something about my words caused her to tighten on my manhood. “Come for me, Norah. Come for Daddy. You know you want to feel me release inside you.”

“You feel so good,” she mumbled, her words slurring.

“Are you coming?”

Norah nodded.

“Not without me.” I flipped her over, placing her back on the couch, putting me on top. My hips thrust faster as her screams of ecstasy filled my office. Stroking deeper, I wanted to make sure she never forgot just who the fuck I was. “Tell me again,” I demanded as my grip tightened on her hips, holding her body right where I needed her. "Tell me, Norah. Give me the words."

"I love you, Cade."

Her body released around me, wetness covering every inch of me. But did I stop? Hell no. I wanted more. When I was in my office, I wanted to look over at this couch and remember the moment she became mine. "Norah," I mumbled into her neck as I felt my orgasm rushing up, the force of my release was so strong, it felt as if I were floating. As my warmth entered her, she arched her back, wetness raining down her channel once again. Norah whimpered, her hands clawing at my shirt.

"God woman, I fucking love you." I shifted to the side, removing most of my weight from her body. It was a tight fit, but I pulled her close enough for us to make it work.

“Promise me something,” she said with a smile on her face and her eyes still closed.

Hell, this woman could have everything I had to give, and then some. “Whatever you want.”

Turning, she draped one bare leg over my half-clothed lower body. Once she got her bearings, she’d fuss at me for still wearing most of my clothes while she was naked.

“Promise me it’ll always be like this with us. Even with kids and life and when I’m wrinkled, and things aren’t as perky as they are now.”

Laughing, I squeezed her ass with one hand before using the other hand to lift her chin. “My feelings for you will never change. Even when we’re old and gray, my love for you is blind to anything and anyone else. Now, why don’t we go home and finish what we started?”

“We have three hours until Lilly gets home. Race you.” She hopped up, running over to her clothes as I sat up slowly. Damn, how did I get so lucky?

Epilogue

Norah

One Year Later

"Cade, it's time. Wake up."

His eyes opened slowly. But once he got a good luck at my face, he smiled. "Is it time?"

Breathing heavily, I tried to focus on anything other than the pain working its way through my body.

"Yes. I need to take a shower," I rolled to the side of the bed and moved to get up, but he was already standing in front of me.

"What are you doing? We're going to the hospital. There's no time for the shower."

Don't ask me why, but I immediately burst into tears. It wasn't fair that I couldn't take a shower before having his big-headed baby. For a first child, the doctor said I would probably be a week or two late. Nope, I had to be different.

Rather, little Adam had to be different.

Apparently, he was so damn big that I was going into labor a week early.

Thank God my mom was staying with us. So was Elizabeth. My dad was at home. We were supposed to call him when his new grandbaby decided to make an entrance. Cade's parents were older and had stayed away for now. They would be coming to the house once the baby and I were back at home and settled.

"Norah. Baby, stop crying. If you want to have a shower first, that's fine. How about I have one with you? We can shower together and that way it'll go faster."

I slapped his hands away and tried my best to walk fast… more like waddle… toward the bathroom. "No. This is all your fault anyway. First, you get me pregnant with your big-headed baby and then we had sex last night. My momma told you what might happen, but could you wait? No, you couldn't. So, now I'm not talking to you. Go shower in another room." Slamming the door to the bathroom, I immediately opened it again. "I'm sorry."

He was still standing there, looking so patient, sexy, and understanding… and did I say sexy? Just as he always did.

"I love you, Norah. I'm glad you're having my big-headed baby and making me a father for a second time and giving Lilly a little brother to love."

See, this is why I loved him. Maybe I didn't deserve him, but he was mine. I wasn't giving him up and no one could make me. "I love you, too. Um… Can you help me with my shower? I can't bend over to reach my legs." Once I hit my ninth month, my stomach got so big, I couldn't do a lot of things. We'd taken to showering together every day. Sighing at the thought, I felt overcome by emotions. "Cade? Are you happy?"

He'd finished turning on the shower when I asked him that question. "What?"

"Are you happy? I mean, we got married after we found out I was pregnant. Your life changed so much in such a short time."

"Stop, Norah. Yes, I'm happy. You and Lilly and little Adam are my life. My world. There's nothing I want more than to be your husband and father to our children. I already told you, I want as many babies as you're willing to give me. Even when you look like you're carrying twins and there's only one big-headed baby inside you."

I nodded. "I'm happy, too. My life couldn't be any better. You're an amazing husband and father and we're so lucky to have you." I paused, feeling another tightening of my stomach. When it passed, I stopped procrastinating and began getting undressed. It was time to get to the hospital. "You better have me a push gift," I muttered.

"Aren't I all the gift you need?"

"You wish," I said with a smile, but in all honesty, he had a point. He was the best gift I could have ever received.

Twelve hours later, I was exhausted but happy. They'd placed me in a large private room that I knew wasn't the standard issue. When we toured the hospital and they'd shown us the recovery room, Cade had been displeased at the size and that I might have a roommate. He must have pulled some strings and made other arrangements for me.

Adam Cade Donovan weight nine pounds eight ounces. He was our little chunky butt, and I couldn't be happier. When things started happening down there, I thought Cade would leave and let my mother inside. No dice.

He was with me the entire time, holding my hand, encouraging me, and telling me how much he loved me for giving him the gift of another child.

The door opened and my mother walked in with a balloon bouquet in her hand. "My baby. How are you feeling?"

"I'm fine, momma."

"I love you, Norah, but I was talking to my grandbaby Adam." She smirked at me, making that outlandish statement. "I'm kidding." She came over to hug me. "I'm so proud of you. He's a beautiful baby."

"Thanks momma. Where's Daddy?"

"Parking the car. Elizabeth stayed home with Lilly but they're gonna be here in the next hour or so. We wanted to make sure you had a chance to recuperate before she came. You know how excited she is for her little brother."

I smiled, overcome with emotion at all the support from our families. "Thanks, mom."

The door swung open and in came Cade with a bag of food. The hospital food would have been just fine for me, but again, my man had to be extra. “Hey, baby.”

“Hey, sweetheart. Hi momma Bernice.”

“Hiya, Cade.”

I sat up when he started removing food from the bags. “Are you planning to feed an army?”

“You need to eat to regain your strength. Plus, there’s me, your mom, your dad, Elizabeth, Robert, and Lilly, and we all need to eat.” Pausing, he walked over to me. “Sweetheart, you’ve done an amazing job bringing our son into the world. Let me do the rest.” Leaning down, he kissed me softly. “I love you.”

I’m not even going to think about how ratchet I probably looked right now. At least I’d been smart enough to get my hair braided a few weeks ago. There was no way in hell I was going to try and wrangle my hair while also worrying about giving birth.

Shortly afterwards, the room began to fill up with guests. My daddy finally arrived, then Elizabeth, Robert, and Lilly.

"Mommy Norah, where's my brother," she announced as soon as she walked into the room.

"Hey, Ladybug. Come here," I held out my arms to her and Cade helped her climb up on the bed with me. My mom brought Adam over from his bassinet and placed him in my arms. "Lillian Annette Donovan, meet your little brother Adam Cade Donovan. He's so happy to meet you."

Her face was filled with awe as she stared down at the bundle in my arms.

"Hi Adam. I'm your big sister." She reached out to touch one of his tiny fingers. "I'm gonna take care of you."

I glanced up and my gaze captured Cade's as he stood behind Lilly. "I think she just claimed him." I couldn't help the small laugh that escaped. "I'll help you with Adam and so will your dad."

Lilly shook her head at me. "No, momma Norah. He's my baby. I got it." I couldn't help the laugh that escaped. Lilly was trying to take over my baby. I looked up at Cade, a smile hovering on my lips. "Um…."

He smiled down at me. "Let her have this moment and we'll deal with it later. For now, I want you to focus on getting some rest."

Nodding, I looked at the family surrounding me. My heart was so full of love, I knew this is where I was supposed to be. Touching Cade on the arm, I lifted my face for a kiss. When we broke apart, I whispered, "Thank you."

He shook his head. "No. Thank you, sweetheart. You're amazing. I had no idea how much I could love you until you came into my life. I will do everything in my power to make you happy." He paused, still looking down at me. "You are so beautiful."

"Love really is blind because that's a whole dang lie." I was trying to watch my language since my two babies were in the room. "But I love you for saying it though."

"It's the truth," he said with a smirk.

I had no idea what life had in store for us, but I knew it was up to me to build my own happiness. Sometimes, when I'm alone, I still thought about my desperate letter to The Love Vixen all those months ago. She told me that grief takes time, that everyone has their own timetable to move on to the next phase of their life. It may have taken me a while to get where I needed to be, but I wouldn't change a thing.

Rebecca was no longer alive, but she was still here with us, in the face of her daughter, in some of the simple touches of our home. So when I said I wasn't trying to replace her, it was true. But in the process, I found my own place and now that I was here, I would live my best life with the man I loved by my side.

~FIN~

****Disclaimer.* The Love Vixen is a fictional character. She is not a doctor, and her advice should probably never be followed. Anything resembling an actual event or article is completely ridiculous because I made the whole thing up!

Ready for More Love Vixen Books?

If this is your first Love Vixen book, check out the entire series here: The Love Vixen.

Let's Talk Love by Lizabeth Scott
Lust or Love by Jeannette Winters
Getting Lucky In Love by Dylann Crush
A Warrior To Love by J.M. Madden
Bone Frog Love by Sharon Hamilton
One Of A Kind Love by Christina Tetreault
Mistaken For Love by Delancey Stewart
Silver Lining Love by Melanie Shawn
Deadline For Love by Jade Webb

Blinded By Love by Reana Malori
Waiting For Love by Lacey Black
My Bet's On Love by Lizabeth Scott

Wouldn't you like to be a Vixen too?
Join our private and interactive Facebook Group or Party Central as we like to call it:
https://www.facebook.com/groups/TheLoveVixN

Don't miss any of the Love Vixen's year of release celebrations!
Sign up for The Love Vixen Newsletter:
https://bit.ly/TheLoveVixen

Thank You!

Thank you for supporting my writing. It truly means a lot to me. If you enjoyed **Blinded by Love**, Cade and Norah's story, please take a few moments to leave a review on the platform where this book was purchased.

As you may know, reviews help motivate authors as we continue writing and bringing you great stories. The more reviews on a book, the more visible it becomes to other readers.

Thank you for your support!

* * * * *

Keep swiping to read an excerpt from Ruthless Bachelor.

Ruthless Bachelor
Summary

People say I don't have a heart…or a soul. That I'm not capable of caring about anyone but myself. They're wrong. I love my family, even my troublemaker little brother. Women? Meh, not so much. I learned the hard way to never confuse my heart with my dic… well, you get it.

I have the perfect life. I answer to no one and everything I do is on my terms. Nothing gets in the way of what I want, and yes, that includes women. I've had countless attractive women in my bed, for a night, but never more than that.

Heads up ladies, I have very special skills that women crave, but I'm a one and done with you kinda guy. Don't give me your number. I won't be calling you. Names are optional. I'll probably forget it anyway. I'm not a complete ass about it, I always make sure to have a car waiting in the morning.

And then Anya walks into my neat, compartmentalized life and now the jokes on me. One taste of her and I want more. Need more. Crave more. Does Anya really believe that she can deny me? Hasn't anyone told her that I play dirty? I'm not going anywhere because I know I have what she can't resist. One problem, she seems to hold the same power over me. My name is Hunter but I might just have become the prey.

One

Hunter

Sipping my favorite scotch, I looked around at all the single women mixing and mingling, playing their nightly game of 'Catch a Bachelor.' If only these women knew the truth, they'd probably run for the front door as fast as they could. Every single man in this room could be described as an Apex Predator, myself included. We didn't play fair. We played to win. And tonight, winning the game meant getting the hottest, most beautiful woman in the room to take a ride in the elevator upstairs to our expensive apartment.

Just thinking about the possibilities in store for tonight brought a smile to my face. I took another sip and watched as one of my buddies strolled through the crowd, making his way over to me. A half-smile tilted my lips as I watched him get closer.

"Hunter," he greeted, sitting in the chair across from me.

"Bryce," I returned, lifting my glass in a mock toast.

His gaze flitted around the packed room of people before he turned back to me. "Full house tonight."

"Yup," I agreed. This bar was the place to be. The luxury could not be hidden or denied. Living here was the ultimate sign of success, and I deserved every bit of the life I'd created for myself.

"Yeah, this place is a damn smorgasbord of beautiful women," he said, winking at a woman walking past us. "Plus, you know how it is in here when the sun goes down. The food isn't the only buffet laid out for us to sate our appetite. It's been a long ass week, and I'm ready for some fun."

Usually, I agreed with him, but I was feeling off-kilter this evening. There was something in the air, and I wasn't sure how to explain it. "I'm not even sure why I'm down here tonight. It's been a long fucking week. I just want to relax, not deal with this game." I could feel a headache growing behind my eyes. I'd been in the middle of negotiations for two weeks working on a purchase from a small information technology company. They had software I needed to expand my business to better support my federal government clients. This deal could not fail. If it did, there would be significant ramifications for my company.

Pinching my fingers against my temple, I tried to hold off the pain making its way through my head. The company knew they had me over a barrel because my Chief Technology Officer let it slip that our government contracts were as good as dead without their software. I might just fire his ass on Monday.

Now, because of his fuck-up, I had to come up with a new strategy to help the owners understand this wasn't a deal they should pass up. I'd offered them a sweet deal, but they needed to get on board.

My fist clenched as I thought of my CTO's fuckup. It would serve his ass right if I made a few calls and made sure he never worked in the northeast again. My anger and frustration at his reckless slip of the tongue weren't going away any time soon. I needed something to take the edge off. Maybe I needed to take a page from Bryce's playbook and get lost between the legs of a buxom blonde or brunette.

Bryce lifted his feet and placed them on the table in front of him. Rude? Yes. Then again, it wasn't my building. If there was a problem with what he was doing, someone would speak up. Then again, with how much we paid to live here, maybe they wouldn't.

"Did you wrap up that acquisition?" He asked, his gaze tracking the women around the room, trying to identify his prey for the night.

Shaking my head, I placed my drink on the table beside me before learning forward. "No. I have a feeling I'm going to spend more on this deal than I thought." And just the thought of that frustrated me even more.

"Is it too late to walk away?"

There was no easy answer to that question. On the one hand, I wanted to wash my hands of this whole thing. Contracts with the government always came with a load of bullshit extras. Picking up my drink and taking another sip, I felt the burn down my throat and let it calm the fire inside me.

"At this point, I wish I could. There's some real momentum behind what they're doing with their software. This is a gamechanger for me." I shook my head. "No. It's too late to walk away." I could feel my jaw clenching. "This shit was supposed to wrap up two days ago. If I don't get what the fuck I want, heads are gonna roll."

"Damn, man. What are you going to do?"

Leaning back in my seat, I reached over and picked up my drink before answering. "I'm going to win. That's what I do. There's no other option."

Laughing, Bryce nodded. "Yes. Yes, winning is definitely what you do. Just don't ruin anyone's life in the process."

I glared at him. "What the fuck are you talking about?" I knew, but I wondered if he was brave enough to say it.

"As if you didn't know that your name on the street is the Grim Reaper. Try that 'I don't know what you're talking about' shit with someone else. You don't have to upend someone's entire life just because you want what they have." He took another sip of his drink as he stared at me, his eyes crinkling at the corners.

"Asshole," I gritted out, which made him chuckle.

"Right back at you. Now," Bryce exclaimed, finally removing his feet from the table, "what kind of trouble are we getting into tonight?"

"I'm not seeing anyone worth the trouble," I respond.

Here's a bit of truth serum from me, which I know isn't always well received. I don't do well with people looking to latch on to someone who can help them get a leg up in this world. No, don't take that the wrong way.

I'm not saying people don't deserve to get rewarded for hard work, dedication, loyalty, or any other word you can add to the mix. On the other hand, I distance myself from people who come off as needy and desperate. Their only focus on life is to latch on to someone else and ride their coattails. Those are the kind of people I walked away from as fast as I can.

Here's the thing, if you can't make it on your own, then I don't want you around me. That's not my game and I can do without the trouble. My little brother, Caleb, tells me I have a fucked-up view of people. Yeah, maybe I do. Then again, he and I grew up in a family dynamic as fucked up as any sob story. Our father was a mean drunk and regularly abused our mother. Our mother was a saint. She deserved so much more than the life she had with our father, taking his abuse for too many years to count. Even though she was hurting and struggling to deal with the pain he put her through, she tried to instill the right morals and values into Caleb and me. Ones like kindness, charity, empathy. All the things that made a person weak and prone to manipulation.

Thank God neither my brother nor I followed that path.

Bryce's voice broke through my inner musings. "I see we have some new visitors to the Tower." His eyes were focused on the entrance to the large bar area.

A little about this place, which we fondly referred to as the Bachelor Tower. This place caters to men. Single men. Wealthy Men. No kids. No women. No animals. Well, women and animals were allowed if they were escorted by a resident.

This place was meant for us. It was all ours, and it was perfect. We had a lounge/bar that served the best scotch, whiskey, or whatever your preferred drink. It also had a fully equipped gym, a sauna to release the tension, and yes… even a cigar lounge for those who occasionally enjoyed a good toke after a long day closing multi-million-dollar deals.

Safe haven didn't even begin to explain the feeling of this place. It was so much more than that.

The one exception to the no-woman rule was the bar. Women could come and go as they pleased, but they could not go beyond these walls without an escort. It was a hard and fast rule of the Tower. And as far as I know, everyone abided. There'd been talk of allowing women to live here, but from what I'd heard, that hadn't gone over very well. Hell, the only reason I had my apartment here was because my mentor had it first. When he found a woman to marry, he moved out. I was the first person he called about moving in. It was all hush-hush since getting into this place was like getting entry into a secret society. An invitation to move into Bachelor Tower was almost invaluable.

But, hell, I wasn't looking a gift horse in the mouth, but I also knew without my mentor, they wouldn't have let me within thirty feet of the front door. Didn't matter how much money I had in my bank account. To move into the Tower, there are extensive background checks. And let's just say, my background ain't squeaky clean. In fact, it's pretty much black and gray from some of the shit I've done in my past and the people who helped me get a leg up.

See, I know what it's like to be at the bottom, but my pride and ego wouldn't let me stay there.

Turning my gaze to where Bryce was looking, my eyes homed in on the vision in front of me, and everything around me stopped. Including the breath in my lungs. My drink was halfway to my mouth when my hand paused. I couldn't take my eyes off her.

Goddamn, she was beautiful. This was definitely a woman I wanted to know better.

Laughter met my ears, but I didn't turn to look at Bryce. "You can't have her," he said. His tone was light, but I wasn't in a playing mood. "I saw her first, and I plan on doing bad things with her all night."

"I can't have who?" Even I could hear the deadly growl in my voice. I don't know why I felt a surge of jealousy as I looked at the woman walking with her friend. If Bryce thought he would push me out of the way and stop me from getting what I wanted, he'd better think again.

"The blonde, of course."

My head whipped around. "Of course?" I couldn't help but question his words. Did he miss the stunning creature walking next to the blonde? Legs a mile long. Body like a country backroad. Wavy hair hung down her back. Full, lush lips. Nah, I didn't want the blonde. Watching her walk closer to me, well, closer to the bar, I knew my night had just gotten much more interesting.

Bryce opened his big mouth again. "Yeah, you have to find your own woman tonight."

I ignored Bryce and his inconsequential words. That he'd passed over and dismissed the beauty walking next to the blonde was unfortunate. Then again, his preference wasn't my concern. My gaze tracked her every move. I watched her smile at the bartender as he took her drink order. My pants tightened at the thought of having her beneath me. Yeah, things were beginning to look up in my world.

Calling over a waiter walking by, I told him what I wanted. He nodded and walked off to take care of my request.

"What did you just do?" Bryce asked, a frown on his face.

"Don't worry about me. You can have your chosen woman. She doesn't entice me in the least. I have... someone else who's caught my attention." Tipping my drink at my friend, I stared across the room as things played out. If everything went to plan, I would be having an exceptionally good night.

* * *

Ruthless Bachelor is Now Available for your reading pleasure!

ReanaMalori

About the Author

USA Today bestselling author Reana Malori pens gripping multicultural/interracial contemporary romance novels full of love, steam, and suspense that will pull you into her world. You'll want to run away with these smoking hot book boyfriends and find a happily ever after alongside heroines you'd love as a best friend. Grab a glass of wine and enjoy!

Reana began her writing journey in 2009, releasing her first novella, To Love a Marine. Since then, she has published more than 40 books, to include Weekend Fling, Finding Faith, Odin's Honor, and Secret Devotion. She currently resides in Montclair, Virginia with her husband and two sons who keep her busy laughing, having fun, and making sure she doesn't take herself too seriously.

Love and Hugs,
Reana Malori ♥

Also by Reana Malori

****

Blinded by Love (The Love Vixen)
Claiming Lana
Closer to You
Conall (Irish Sugar)
Desperado
Finding Faith
Flawless (F'd Up Fairy Tales)
Losing Control
Promise Me
Queen of Spades (The Player's Club)
Ruthless Bachelor (Bachelor Towers)
Salvation: The Italian's Story
Secret Devotion
Shame the Devil
Spellbound
Stay With Me
Tangled Lies
The Long Shot
Three Wishes
To Love a Marine
Unwrapping a Marriage (w/ Michel Prince)
What Matters Most
Whip Appeal
Workout Partners

Angel Hearts

Dark Angel (Book 1)
Broken Angel (Book 2)
Raven's Crown

Absolution

Bloodmoon Pack

Odin's Honor

Heaven on Earth

Escape to Heaven (Book 1)

Redemption (Book 2)

Sacrifice (Book 3)

Homecoming (Book 4)

Lady Guardians

Forgiven (Book 1)

Persuade Me (Book 2)

Lunchtime Chronicles

The Nooner

Red Light Special

Blackberry Pie

Second Chances

Second Chances (Book 1)

Renewal (Book 2)

Weekend Lovers

Weekend Fling (Book 1)

Weekend Rendezvous (Book 2)

Wicked Nights - A Collection of Sexy Shorts

Change of Heart

Need You Tonight

Night in Heaven
Praline Dreams
Shadow Mates
Taylor's Gift

Decadent Delights: A Collection of Steamy Shorts
Accepting the Dragon
Dinner for Three
Hidden Depths
Naughty Nanny
Holiday Desire

Made in the USA
Monee, IL
04 September 2023